The Wrong Husband

B.M. Hardin

T0204374

Copyright©2015

David Weaver Presents/Savvily Published LLC

ISBN-13: 978-0692597088

ISBN-10: 0692597085

Dedication

This book is dedicated to a few special superstar readers, Kimberly Miller, Cassie Garcia, Shekie Johnson, Muriel Holloway, and Felica Turner.

Thank you all for your support and for following me on my writing journey. It is truly a blessing to have supporters like you in my corner. Thank you!

Acknowledgements

First and foremost, I want to thank my Heavenly Father for my talents and my gifts and each and every story that he has placed in me.

It is an honor and a privilege to be living my dream and walking in my purpose and for that I am forever thankful.

Also to all of my family, friends, critiques, supporters, readers and everyone else, thank you for believing in me and allowing me to share my gifts with you.

Your support truly means the world to me!

B.M. Hardin

Author B.M. Hardin's contact info:

Facebook: http://www.facbook.com/authorbm

Twitter: @BMHardin1

Instagram: @bm_hardin

Email:bmhardinbooks@gmail.com

The Wrong Husband

CHAPTER 1

One Mississippi, Two Mississippi, Three Mississippi…

By the time that I'd gotten to fifty, Eddie grunted, released himself inside of me, and collapsed onto the bed.

Again?

You have got to be kidding me!

After glancing under the covers at my frustrated vagina, I mugged my husband and envied the stupid grin of satisfaction on his face.

Eddie mumbled good night and I responded with a groan.

He immediately started to snore, and I wondered what he would do if I just hauled off and punched him in the face.

I swear I balled up my fists and everything.

This was the second time this week that he'd *gotten him*, and I didn't even half way get me.

How selfish could he be?

Hell, what woman could cum in just fifty seconds?

Tell me, how is that possible?

If there was a woman that could, I wish someone would ask her if I could borrow her coochie for the remainder of my marriage.

Tell her to help a sista' out or something!

With his snores filling up the empty spaces of the room, I smacked my lips and forced myself to ignore the *whines* of the "unsatisfied woman" that lived in between my thighs, and I turned my back to my husband.

Mr. Cum Fast A lot…and I was going to call him that in the morning too!

The next morning I woke up with an attitude, but I had things to do.

Being that I had woken up late, I rushed out of the house greeting the winds of the brisk Saturday morning and sped to pick up my friend.

I was already in a bad mood and she just seemed to make it worse.

I should have never agreed to take her.

"Don't get mad at me because you're all married with kids, and boring these days," Patrice laughed.

I rolled my eyes.

Patrice was my sister from another mother.

She wasn't my biological sister; but we were as close as two butt cheeks.

Well, at least we used to be.

Here lately, she was always on the go; traveling and experiencing the world.

It seemed as though I saw less and less of her as the years went by and in a way, I envied her freedom and her ability to live life worry free and without restraints.

We'd planned to enjoy that type of life together, but I never got the chance to.

I got married instead.

"Shut up. I love my family. I just woke up on the wrong side of the bed this morning. And as for you, I'm just saying. You're always going somewhere, or doing something. Dang, stay at home sometime."

"Nope. I'm going to enjoy my life. You only live once as they say. I worked hard for the past fifteen years and now I'm free. And let me tell you, there is nothing like being and feeling free."

"Yeah, I guess so. But maybe it's time to get married and have some kids."

"No thanks. From the looks of it, I'm never getting married. And I'll probably never have kids either. And I'm okay with that. Marriage is for suckers. I don't mean no harm, but married folks are some of the most miserable people that I have ever met. And you know that I'm telling the truth," she laughed.

"Maybe some are. But you can't say that about every married person Patrice. You definitely can't say that about me. I'm not miserable."

"Oh really?"

"Really."

"Whatever you say girl."

She blew me a kiss, winked her eye and got out of my car in a hurry.

She didn't have long to get to where she was going inside of the airport in order to make her flight.

I watched her until I couldn't see her anymore, and then I finally drove away.

I had a feeling that one day she was going to board one of those planes and never come back.

I wouldn't be surprised one bit if she did.

Patrice's family had money.

Her father was a movie producer and her mother had owned her own clothing line; which Patrice had taken over and started to run once her mother passed away.

After many years, Patrice finally realized that the clothing line was her mother's dream…not hers.

Though she had taken it to the next level and it had become an even bigger success, she decided that she just didn't want to do it anymore.

She wanted to live out her dreams instead.

So, Patrice sold the entire clothing line for big bucks and ever since then she had been doing what she loved.

But despite that, the Patrice that I've known for well over twenty years had always dreamed of the perfect husband and a house full of kids.

So she could pretend to not want it all she wanted to.

I knew her.

And besides, Patrice had it all wrong.

Marriage is a beautiful thing.

She wished that she had a husband and kids to go home to like I did. I don't care how much she tried to hide it.

And she was wrong about me.

I wasn't miserable.

I was happy.

Sometimes.

Kind of.

Most of the time.

Uh oh…

~***~

On everything that I love, today is not the day for this!

"Who in the hell is this?"

They just sat there and breathed on the other end of the phone, just like they always did.

Whoever the idiot was had been calling, repeatedly, for the past couple of days, and they were getting on my last damn nerve!

They never said a word and if they knew like I knew, they had better utilize that voice of theirs because if I ever found out who they were, I was going to try my best to kick their voice box out of their throat!

"Don't call my phone again if you're not going to say anything."

Who in heck invented Private Calling?

I desperately wanted to find out who just so I could call them private and curse them the hell out!

Just as I moved the phone away from my ear, finally, the person on the other end spoke.

They were whispering so I pressed the phone up against my left ear and placed my index finger in my right one to suppress the noise in the background.

"I love you," they whispered.

What?

I could tell that it was a man's voice but that was about it.

"Who is this? Eddie is that you? Why are you playing on my phone?"

I waited for a response but they didn't say anything else.

Instead, they hung up.

I shook my head and managed to smile.

Eddie, my husband, must have been playing some kind of crazy prank.

He was the only man that would be calling me saying that he loved me, so I was sure that it was him.

I actually found it kind of cute since he hadn't done anything silly in a long time, and since he acted like he was always so damn busy.

He was definitely not the man that he used to be.

And that wasn't a good thing.

I turned my phone on silent, placed it in my purse and headed into work.

Another day, another dollar.

Now let's get this day over and done with...

"We need to have some fun," I said to Eddie later on that evening.

"We have fun all the time."

I looked at Eddie.

What was he smoking?

We hardly ever did anything fun these days.

Sure, he made me laugh, occasionally, but that was about it. And that wasn't exactly what I would call fun.

"No we don't, but we should."

"Well, plan something and I'm there," he said.

I actually did have something in mind and I was happy that he was onboard.

"You wanna do something after dinner? What about a board game?"

"No. Not tonight. Maybe a movie."

A movie wasn't fun but I nodded.

I guess I shouldn't be complaining.

At least he did want to spend some kind of quality time with me.

"Oh, Eddie, I meant to ask you this earlier. Have you been playing on my phone?"

"No. Why would I play on your phone?"

"I don't know. Someone has been calling non-stop for the past few days and finally they whispered and said "I love you" today."

"Let me find out you have a stalker. Is there someone I need to know about huh?"

I shook my head.

"Yeah right."

Eddie laughed and walked away.

I was faithful, but boy was he pushing it.

And if he wasn't the one playing on my phone then who was?

Maybe they had the wrong number or something, especially since they'd said that they loved me.

I guess I had spoken it into the atmosphere, because suddenly my phone started to ring and the word "Private" displayed across the screen.

Ugh!

I was going to have to change my damn number, or folks were going to start thinking that I had a bad case of Tourette syndrome because I every time they called I screamed and cursed them out before I would even answer it.

Leaving it ringing and unanswered on the couch, I walked away and headed to prepare dinner for my family.

~***~

"What are you looking at Polo?" I quizzed my husband's best friend.

He appeared to be staring at me, causing me to look down at myself to make sure that everything was intact.

He started to laugh like a lunatic and poured himself another drink.

But he kept his eyes on me the whole time.

"What is it silly? What are you looking at?"

He smiled.

"You."

That was it.

That was all that he said as he strolled away.

He was such a weirdo.

To me, Polo always seemed to have had a few screws loose.

But I seemed to be the only one that noticed it.

He was always the life of the party but in a crazy unstable kind of way, yet you couldn't help but enjoy his company.

He was just one of those people that everyone wanted to be around, or maybe it was that he needed to be around people to keep him balanced.

Either way, there was never a dull moment with him in the room.

And I knew that after a while and after a few more drinks, he was going to contribute to making this night epic.

I shrugged my shoulders and headed back to the living room with my husband's birthday cake.

I'd planned a surprise party for him and the turnout was better than I'd expected.

At the sight of me and the cake, everyone started to sing happy birthday and Eddie approached me with a smile on his face.

He'd just turned thirty-five but he didn't look a day older than twenty.

When they'd said that *black don't crack*...they'd meant it.

Whether talking about a man or a woman.

He was one of the sexiest black men that I'd ever seen.

Average height, brown-skinned, and he looked as though he hadn't aged a day since the very first time that I'd laid eyes on him.

For the most part, I was proud to be his wife, and maybe even a little bit lucky.

At least from the outside looking in.

"Happy birthday babe," I kissed him right after he blew out his candles.

"Thank you. Now cut the cake so we can get these people out of my house, and the real party can begin," he said with a sly grin and slightly patted me on my booty.

I smiled back at him as I said a quick prayer in my head.

"Please let him last longer than two minutes this time. Or I just might have to cut him. Amen."

Don't get me wrong, I loved my husband.

And I mean I absolutely adored Eddie.

He was so good to me and he always had been.

But his sex was horrible these days!

I had no idea as to what had happened to my freaky-spontaneous- get me right-every single night-husband, but I missed him like crazy!

Hell maybe the old him had been abducted by aliens or something.

And if that was the case, who did I have to sleep with in order for them to bring him back?

Just thinking about how everything had changed pissed me off. And if it wasn't fixed soon, I was going to go insane.

Sex with Eddie was so boring that I'd rather be working or cleaning, or pretty much doing anything else than laying there with him on top of me for two minutes or less.

It was just a waste of my time.

Most of the time the only way that I received a decent orgasm was when it was from his mouth or from my hand.

Every blue moon his penis would get the job done but it was so rare that I couldn't even remember the last time that I'd been satisfied from penetration.

Seriously, it was just that bad.

Sex had simply become a duty and I for one, didn't appreciate it; especially because I knew how it could be and how it used to be.

Of course it hadn't always been this way.

I wouldn't have married him if it had.

We used to have some headboard banging, semi-stalking him, type of sex.

If I remembered correctly, it was around the time that he'd started his own accounting firm, that the bedroom side of things started to suffer.

At first I'd thought that it was because of me.

In the ten years that we'd been together, I must say, I'd put on a good bit of weight; especially around the hips and thighs.

But then I noticed that Eddie touched me every chance that he could, so I was sure that it wasn't that.

From the looks of it, he liked the extra meat on my bones.

So, the only thing that I could think of was that maybe it was stress from work, or the added pressure of trying to run a company that had somehow affected his stamina or something.

Maybe it was the fact that he was always so busy, working late, or burnt out from sixty-hour work weeks that his body only had enough fuel to make sure that he got his nut, and then it ran out of gas when it came time for me to get mine.

But Eddie started his own business three years ago and though his company was doing great these days, his sex still sucked!

And I mean it sucked in an eye-rolling, get off of me, I hope he catches a Charley-horse, sucked.

But I forced myself to fake through it.

It was the only thing that I knew to do.

I'd tried to tell him once or twice that things in the bedroom had changed but the words hadn't come out right.

And when he did somewhat get the hint, he blamed it on me and the wetness of my *pu-pu*.

Eddie would say that the feeling always felt so damn good, and that *it* was always so wet, that sometimes he just couldn't control himself.

But that was a bunch BS if you ask me.

I had the same pussy today as I'd had ten years ago, and sex back then between us was always good.

It had my nose so wide open that you could build a four lane highway straight through it.

But now he was lucky that I even opened my legs.

And if I wasn't the blame, he would simply say that he was too tired to last too long or that he was getting old.

So, basically, and simply put: I was shit out of luck.

I was past sexually frustrated, yet, I never denied him of the booty; no matter how bad or how much I wanted to.

And because I loved him so much, I'd convinced myself that I just had to deal with it, until he finally figured out the problem.

But hopefully tonight would be different.

Hell, anything was possible.

I sat the cake down and reached Eddie the knife.

As he started to cut it, I made my way back to the kitchen to refill the bowl of punch.

Now, Polo was sitting on the edge of the counter, drinking himself half-way to death as usual.

"Boy if you don't get your ass off of my counter I'm going to hurt you," I joked with him and he hurriedly jumped down.

Polo and Eddie were as close as brothers and they were the true definition of what best friends were supposed to be.

And everybody knew it too.

I had two best friends, Patrice and Micki, and though we were close, we didn't have a thing on them.

Eddie and Polo had been friends since they were all of five years old and boy could you tell.

They grew up right next door to each other and every memory that one seemed to share, so did the other.

Their bond was so strong that it was damn near suspect; especially if you didn't know them.

Call me silly, but I strongly believed that if Eddie ever had to choose between us: Polo and I, for whatever reason, he might mess around and choose Polo.

Maybe I was exaggerating, but they were just that close .

Closer than any male friends that I'd ever seen.

And I had to say that from being around Polo all of these years, I could see why Eddie was fond of him, in a way.

I guess I could consider Polo a friend too.

I loved him because my husband loved him so much and despite some of his ways, he was a part of our family.

I used to feel like I had to compete with him for my husband's time and attention, but once I figured out that he loved us both, in different ways and on different levels, I quickly adjusted and simply embraced Polo, seeing that it made life a whole lot easier.

Eddie was an only child, so pretty much Polo was the brother that he never had.

But although Eddie and Polo grew up around the same place, at the same school and had even gone to the same college, they couldn't have been more different.

Eddie was conservative, passive, hard-working and so sweet that just by touching him you could get diabetes.

But Polo was the complete opposite.

He was a bit rough around the edges.

He was loud, aggressive and he could be an asshole at times.

He was a walking tornado.

It seemed as though trouble followed him everywhere that he went and if he was in a bad mood, everything in his path was at risk of being destroyed.

I'd seen him in action plenty of times, and even if I wasn't the one that he had an issue with, I had to make sure that I had a weapon within my reach.

Just in case he started flipping out on everybody or something. He would surely mess around and flip into an ass whoopin' coming my way.

But Eddie was the only one that could control him.

Polo had three baby's mamas, two ex-wives, and enough drama and entertainment in his life, regularly, for a soap opera.

But I guess you could expect that from somebody that was rolling in dough.

If money made normal people act funny, you could only imagine how it made someone as unstable and thrown off as Polo act.

Eddie and I were pretty stable, a successful couple and didn't want for anything.

But Polo was one of those people that had more money than he knew what to do with, and quite frankly, more than I felt like he could handle.

Polo invented a sex toy that took over the industry and he'd made millions off of it.

But money, nice cars, a big house and expensive suits, didn't change the man.

He was still the same man inside.

He was always in some kind of trouble and Eddie was always coming to his rescue.

But that's what friends were for I suppose.

And if I had to be honest, Polo was a pretty decent friend to Eddie as well.

If he didn't care about anyone else, he cared about Eddie.

Polo had given Eddie the money to start his business and though Eddie had paid him back every penny, as the company continued to grow, he always mentioned that he couldn't have done any of it without Polo's help.

I personally thought of it as payback for all of the other stuff that Eddie and I had done for him over the years, but of course my opinion didn't matter much when I was talking about his beloved best friend.

"You're wearing the hell out of that red dress," Polo said, interrupting my thoughts and taking a sip of whatever it was in his glass.

I could tell that he was drunk, but that was normal for him.

Polo was always drunk.

"Thanks boy."

"Um what's up under it?"

What?

What did he say?

"What did you say Polo?"

"Oh, I wasn't talking to you. I was thinking about something."

Um huh.

"Oh. Maybe you should lay off of the alcohol for the rest of the night," I said to him.

"Maybe. But what fun would that be?"

Polo walked closer to me.

He was so close to my face that I could taste the alcohol on his breath.

It was vodka.

He breathed heavily.

Surprisingly, I wasn't as uncomfortable as I probably should have been.

Instead, I seemed to be unbothered by the situation and I could tell that he could sense my comfort.

After all, he was almost like a brother to me.

Almost.

"Go sit your drunk behind down somewhere," I said finally as I reached for the bowl.

Polo didn't respond.

He simply smirked and took another sip of his drink.

What's his problem tonight?

He continued to breathe hard, and might I add, familiarly.

Wait a minute…it couldn't be.

But something told me that my hunch was right.

"Have you been playing on my phone Polo?"

He smiled.

"Yep."

Polo always said the most when he was drunk; hell he didn't even have a filter when he wasn't, so I was sure that he was being honest.

"Why?"

"Why what?"

"Why have you been playing on my phone?"

"I was just having a little fun with you," he said.

"Um huh, I'm gonna' whoop your ass if you call my phone playing again! Talking about you love me, boy," I giggled.

"Well, I do love you."

I looked at him.

"Like a sister of course," Polo finished his statement.

I smirked at him and turned to walk away.

I didn't have time for his foolishness tonight.

But I know one thing, he had better not call my damn phone again.

I entered back into the living room to see Eddie letting loose and actually enjoying himself.

Boy did he need it.

He was always so uptight and I just wanted him to relax and enjoy life a little more.

He deserved a break sometimes.

Eddie worked hard and he did above and beyond on a daily basis for me and our sons, and everyone else around him.

He was the man of every woman's dreams…well…except for mine.

Some would say that he was the guy that every woman wanted but didn't know what to do with him once they had him.

They were probably right.

For some reason, I'd always felt like something just wasn't what it should have been between us.

He was a wonderful guy on paper, and even in reality, but something for me had always been missing.

I'd always felt that way.

And my feelings weren't just a result of the terrible sex life that we shared lately.

You know when you know, that you know, that you know that you know, that even if you don't wanna know that you know, that it's something, but you just couldn't put your finger on it?

That's how it had been being married to Eddie.

Some might say that Eddie was perfect.

But I couldn't exactly say that he was perfect for me.

He looked at me and I smiled as though I'd won some kind of prize or something.

Hey, I'd learned the power of a painted smile years ago.

But just because a woman was smiling, that doesn't mean that she's happy.

You have to learn to see past a woman's smile because nine times out of ten, she might just be really good at pretending.

But I could be real with myself even if I couldn't be real with anyone else.

I wasn't happy.

My husband was loyal, faithful, and everything else in between, but deep down I'd always known that I'd settled.

Yeah, that's right, I'd settled and I wasn't ashamed to admit it.

Eddie and I met in my early twenties.

We were only a few years apart and though we were from the same neck of the woods, we'd never crossed paths until one night at a bar.

I was sitting alone, while my best friends, Micki and Patrice, danced with strangers that had been buying them drinks all night.

"Can I buy you a drink?" Eddie had asked.

"I don't drink. This is just pineapple juice," I'd smiled at him.

Immediately and though it was kind of dark, I noticed how attractive he was.

He had all of his teeth, a nice smile, gorgeous eyes and even a nice build and height.

"Well, is this seat taken?"

I'd shaken my head no.

I could tell that he was kind of nervous.

It was almost as though he didn't randomly talk to women too often and I could tell that approaching me had taken every ounce of his courage.

But he'd done it anyway.

That night, I'd found his nervousness and his innocence kind of cute.

Of course he had been there with Polo; which he was hard not to notice due to the fact that he was being loud and getting drunk just like he did today.

He had women all around him and Eddie kept glancing at him to make sure that he was okay.

"What's your name?"

"Sassi."

"Sassi? Is that your real name?"

I remembered grinning at him.

Everyone asked me that.

"It's the name on my birth certificate, so I would have to say yes. I don't know what my mama was thinking," I'd joked.

And from there he introduced himself and we spent the next hour or so chatting and getting to know each other.

He loosened up, just a little, and I'd actually managed to enjoy our conversation.

But it was cut short once Polo got into a brawl with another guy as a result of trying to push up on his woman.

The owner of the bar asked them both to leave, so of course that'd meant that Eddie had to go too.

"I have to get him out of here. But do you mind if I called you sometime?"

And that was the beginning of Eddie and I.

Dating Eddie had been refreshing.

Immediately I knew that he was different.

I was only around twenty-three at the time, but I'd had my share of no-good men, bad dates, *hit it and quit it* type of guys, so I knew that with Eddie I was getting something different.

Something better.

He was sweet, charming, and so much more.

He opened doors, pulled out chairs, complimented me, and to me, at the time, it just didn't get any better than that.

Eddie still believed in respecting a lady and courting a woman and I liked the idea of having such a mature man in my back pocket.

And after two years, hesitantly, I made my way down the aisle towards him.

I'd had a few feelings before the wedding but back then, I'd thought that they were just pre-wedding jitters and that I was just getting cold feet.

So, I shook it off and I married Eddie anyway.

Intuition is a persistent little bitch ain't she?

So many times we tell *her* to be quiet, when really the best thing for us to do is listen.

I wish that I had.

Immediately after the wedding, I questioned my decision.

I even mentioned my feelings to my mama but she'd only said that I was scared of forever and that it was normal for me to feel that way.

But there was nothing normal about feeling like you may have just made the biggest mistake of your life on your wedding day.

I had no business listening to her old tail anyway.

I should have listened to my heart.

But Eddie had everything, every woman needed so I figured that something was wrong with me.

For years I'd looked over the small stuff and once our first son came into the picture, I knew that it was best to lock those feelings behind a door in my heart and throw away the key.

And that's just what I'd done.

I had my king and he treated me like a queen, and I just became thankful that he'd chosen me.

I was one of the few married woman that I knew of that had a wonderful, faithful husband and a pair of amazing kids to match; and for those two reasons alone, I'd learned to grateful.

But as the years went by, and once the sex became an issue, I started to remember that I wasn't as complete as I pretended to be.

I was just comfortable.

I was just content.

And ten years into this thing, it was too late for me to change my mind.

My kids needed their father, and I wasn't going to take him away from them.

Hell I needed stability and companionship, so I wasn't going to give that up either.

Eddie wasn't just right for me, but he was enough.

And I wasn't letting him go.

And besides, despite it all, I really did love him.

And even though some said that love wasn't enough, for me it just had to be.

It was enough to make me fight.

It was enough to make me believe.

And most importantly, it was enough to make me stay.

"Baby, I love you. Thank you for this," Eddie said disturbing my thoughts.

"Give me a kiss," I said to him and poked out my lips.

I heard him chuckle just before he kissed me and wrapped his arms around me.

My husband.

My protector.

My baby's daddy.

And my friend.

Only the Man above and I knew the whole truth.

Only I knew that Eddie was *the wrong husband*.

But that was just something that I had learned to live with.

Deciding to enjoy the moment, I shook away my thoughts, and I managed to join in on the fun.

"Uh oh, come on sis, let me get a dance in," Polo said, coming out of nowhere.

Generously, Eddie handed me off to his best friend and he started to dance with my friend Patrice, who had made her way back to the country just to celebrate with us.

I shook my head at Polo as the next song started to play, and I laughed at him as he started to dance.

He could barely keep his balance but he was determined on dancing with me no matter what his body was telling him to do.

I danced to the beat, and turned around to cautiously back it up on him.

And that's when I felt it.

I jumped and hurriedly turned back around to face him.

Polo's penis had been so hard that I was sure that it had left some kind of bruise as a result of him grinded it up against my left butt cheek.

"You felt that rock didn't you?" He asked in a whisper.

I looked at him, but he only grinned and walked away.

"Where's he going?" Eddie asked.

I breathed and turned around with a fake smile.

"I don't know. I guess he got tired," I replied and resumed dancing by myself.

What was that all about?

Hours later and as soon as the last guest was out of our driveway, Eddie looked at me with eyes full of lust and I knew what time it was.

Long, passionate sex would have been a great ending to a perfect night but I didn't want to get my hopes up.

At this point I was just hoping to get some type of pleasure out of the whole ordeal.

Eddie locked the front door and grabbed my hand as we ran like teenagers to our bedroom.

He cut on a lamp as I sat on the bed.

Before I could say anything, he pushed me back and I giggled as he tugged at my dress.

"I love you so much Sassi. I really do. These past ten years with you have been like a dream come true. I wouldn't trade you for the world. You, here with me, loving me, and the kids are the only birthday gifts that I needed," Eddie said softly.

See, this is why my ass wasn't going anywhere!

He always had the sweetest, most genuine things to say and the actions to match.

"I love you too," I said to him and I kissed him.

Eddie kissed me, hard, rough, just like he always did when he had a few drinks.

I already knew that he might not last as long as I wanted him too, but I also knew that with alcohol in his system he was going to want to be freaky; which meant that he was going to go *down town* on me.

Translation…I was going to get one heck of an orgasm tonight!

Finally!

Without hesitating, Eddie took off my panties and he kissed different parts of my body until he made his way down to *Pussycat Lane*.

And *she* was waiting for him too.

It had been maybe two weeks since he'd ate my *cookies* and I almost exploded from just the first lick.

Eddie licked, sucked, nibbled and kissed my most valuable possession and I felt as though I was about to lose it.

I held his head firmly in place as I howled to the moon in satisfaction and appreciation.

There was nothing like it.

I started to call him *Daddy* as he licked harder and faster.

My body temperature was way up past normal and I could feel my eyes rolling to the back of my head.

My legs started to shake and I started to curse.

Yes!

Yes!

Wait a minute...

Nooooo!

The noise startled both of us and we both jumped.

"I'm sorry. I thought this was the bathroom," Polo slurred.

What?

What the hell was he still doing here?

Immediately I tried to cover myself and Eddie sat up in front of me.

"Polo I thought you were gone? What are you still doing here?" Eddie asked him.

"I rode here with you remember? You didn't let me drive because you said that I would be drinking. I've been sitting in the backyard for hours. I think I fell asleep for a minute. I had to pee so I came in. Guess I could've have went outside huh? But I was looking for the bathroom. Bro, my bad," Polo said turning his back and staggering out of our bedroom.

Eddie looked at me.

We both seemed to be a little embarrassed.

"Guess I should take him home huh?"

I nodded my head and he helped me to sit up.

"Are you sure you're okay to drive?"

"Oh yeah, I'm fine."

"Okay."

"Finish this when I get back?"

I nodded again as he kissed my forehead and left the room.

Seconds later, I heard the front door close.

What the hell!

Polo was always messing something up!

If he didn't check into rehab soon, I was going to drag him there my damn self!

His drinking was so out of hand!

And he'd just ruined my *happy ending*.

I was definitely in my feelings.

I was so close to a release that I could still feel it in my stomach.

I knew that even if we did *get busy* once Eddie got back home, that it would be one of his little quickies.

The thrill would be gone so I was sure that it would be the normal.

That's if he even felt like fooling around once he got back.

I was so frustrated that I didn't even feel like finishing the *job* myself.

I decided that I might as well clean up some of the mess from the party until Eddie returned.

Wiping off, and changing into something comfortable, I headed out of our bedroom and up the hallway.

As I passed the hallway bathroom, I turned off the light.

I knew that it hadn't been on when Eddie and I had headed to our bedroom only moments before, and I also knew that I hadn't heard Polo stop to use it on their way out.

So who had turned on the light?

Reaching the living room, I started to pick up trash.

And I started to think about Polo's comment.

He'd thought our bedroom was the bathroom my ass!

Damn you Polo!

****

CHAPTER 2

Eddie kissed me and we both headed off to work.

I was an office manager for a huge logistics company.

I enjoyed it.

It wasn't my dream job but I was good at it and I had been doing it for quite some time.

I actually had a thing for journalism, and one day I planned to pursue a career in newspaper or magazine writing.

Or maybe even write a book.

It didn't really matter, as long as I was writing something. Writing was my passion, and I knew that I was good at it and I couldn't wait until it was time for me to show off my skills.

But for now, I was in a good place professionally and honestly, they couldn't survive without me.

And they made sure that I knew it too; my paycheck could vouch for that.

I pulled up at work and to my surprise, I saw Polo sitting there on the hood of his car in a parking space.

I hadn't seen him since Saturday night, at Eddie's birthday party, and I wondered what was so important that he would pop up at my job instead of coming by the house or calling me on the phone.

I even felt as though I wanted to blush as I remembered that he'd walked in on Eddie going down on me.

I didn't think that he'd seen my *cookie jar*, but I couldn't be sure.

But he was drunk so if he did, he probably wouldn't even remember it just like I was sure that he didn't remember getting a hard on from dancing with me or the comment that he had made.

He stood up straight and immediately I noticed his attire.

Polo was impeccable dressed, as always, which was something that I actually liked about him.

But I couldn't help but wonder what he wanted.

"Hey."

"Hey."

"So, I hadn't given Eddie his birthday gift yet, and I have it now for you to give to him."

"Um, why didn't you give it to him yourself? He should be at work by now. Just go take it to him. Why are you giving it to me?"

"Because?"

"Because what?"

"Just because."

He reached me an envelope.

I opened it to find two first class tickets to Hawaii and a few other things pertaining to things that he'd purchased there; such as hotel confirmation, couples spa package and more.

"Aww, he's going to love this!"

"Yeah, I know. He's always wanted to go there. This is for him and for you. As a sorry for my behavior the other night."

I looked at Polo but before I could respond or even thank him, he got into his car and left.

Wow.

I wondered what part he was referring to from the birthday party.

Maybe he was talking about walking in on us or maybe he was pertaining to his behavior towards me.

Either way, this was one hell of a birthday gift!

I couldn't remember the last time that Eddie and I had a vacation, just the two of us, so it was long overdue.

Maybe the change of scenery would spark old flames between us.

Who knows, Eddie might end up *knocking my boots* the way that he used to.

Maybe.

I headed into work and once I got settled, I called Eddie and told him what Polo had done for him; for us.

Of course he questioned why he'd given it to me instead of him but for the most part he was ecstatic.

I loved hearing the excitement in his voice and I loved to see him happy.

And if he was happy, I was happy.

That was the only way I knew how to be.

Thanks Polo.

The best best-friend ever!

~***~

Hawaii was so beautiful that I couldn't really put it into words.

I had never seen water so blue and clear or such beautiful colors and flowers in all of my life.

Eddie squeezed my hand with enthusiasm and we headed for a shuttle to take us to our hotel.

Even the hotel was breathtaking!

I thought about how much Polo had to spend just on the hotel alone.

The room was huge.

It had the biggest king size bed that I'd ever seen and there were fishes swimming around inside of the floor…literally.

Everything was just so perfect.

I heard Eddie on the phone with Polo as I checked out the bathroom.

He thanked him sincerely and my heart smiled.

"Tell him I said thank you too," I chimed.

I was truly thankful that Eddie had someone who loved him even more than I did and enough to give him something that he would never forget.

"I love you."

I kissed Eddie.

He squeezed my booty and immediately his manhood started to swell.

I was all down for seeing if Hawaii had worked some kind of magic on his penis and I was hoping that we were about to have one hell of a good time.

We started to kiss and I became all hot and bothered.

The hairs on the back of my neck stood up and I was becoming aroused like never before.

We were both fully naked in a flash and he laid me on the bed.

We rolled around like crazy, horny teenagers for the next few minutes and if I didn't get some kind of penetration in the next few seconds, my head was going to explode.

This was the Eddie that I remembered.

Thinking about it, the fact that his sex had been so good back then had definitely contributed to me making the decision to go ahead and marry him.

I was definitely sprung.

Eddie had been so good in between the sheets while we were dating and even the first few years of our marriage so I knew that he had it in him.

He just had to figure out how to get back there.

Eddie laid on his back and began to pull on *his pipe*.

"Suck it."

I looked at him.

Now, I didn't mind sucking him off, but it was at my own leisure.

This wasn't cable and it damn sure wasn't on demand!

"Trust me."

I looked at him and figured hell we were in Hawaii, I might as well make the most of every moment, so I did as I was told.

I sucked him for maybe three or four minutes before he filled my mouth with his bitter tasting cum.

I spit out the aftermath of his satisfaction and he started to stroke his penis once again.

He stroked it hard and fast as though he was trying to please himself.

Once it was hard again, he smiled.

"Okay, now, sit on it."

I looked at him with caution, but I straddled him and as soon as it touched the bottom of my stomach, I cooed.

I closed my eyes and started to rock my hips back and forth slowly and with carefulness.

"Ride this thing. Don't be scared," Eddie said and so I picked up the pace.

I couldn't remember the last time that I had been on top and the fact that we were a few minutes into it and he was still in action excited me even more.

Hallelujah!

I rode him hard and thrusted my hips with force, hoping to get to the finish line before he tapped out on me.

But he was hanging in there.

He sat up and flipped me over and got behind me.

He was hitting it from the back too?

Aw hell, did we need to pack up and move to Hawaii for good?

I screamed in pleasure and I was almost scared for the moment to end but the end was coming and with something stirring up inside of me, I couldn't hold back any longer.

I released my creams and only seconds later, Eddie did too.

Breathless, he collapsed and then he rolled over to spoon with me.

I was smiling from ear to ear, and Eddie smiled back at me.

That was one hell of a start to a damn good trip.

We hadn't had sex like that in forever and I was absolutely, the happiest wife in the world at that moment.

"I love you."

"Love you too."

Eddie got up and headed to the bathroom and I thought of what he'd done.

His little stunt had proved that he too noticed that he came too quickly, too often, so he tried a different approach.

I guessed I'd said it without having to say it.

But thank goodness he finally noticed.

If I had to suck him first every single time then you could call me Lock Jaw Sally from now on, as long as that meant that I was going to get something out of the deal.

Getting out of my thoughts, I joined him in the shower and soon after we headed out to enjoy ourselves and all of the different activities that Polo had planned for us.

Later that evening, as we enjoyed our dinner by the beach, I let Eddie talk me into drinking.

Even though I didn't drink, and hadn't even had a sip of alcohol in years, I was on vacation, with my wonderful husband, in Hawaii, so I figured why not.

We'd both had a few drinks too many, but I sure that I wasn't seeing things.

I blinked twice and then I closed my eyes for only a second and then looked again.

Polo.

I lifted up my sunglasses.

Hell yeah, that was him alright.

What the hell was he doing in Hawaii?

He noticed me, noticing him.

He knew that I saw him but he simply grinned at me and turned around and walked away.

He had been watching us in a distance and I wasn't sure how long he'd been there before he'd caught my attention.

"Baby what's wrong?"

I placed my sunglasses back down and continued to watch Polo until he was out of sight.

Polo was getting stranger by the minute, and I was starting to get a little concerned.

"Nothing is wrong baby. Nothing at all."

~***~

It was all too good to be true.

And now I had to walk around with exhausted jaws too.

We'd gotten lucky, twice in Hawaii, with Eddie's little blow job before penetration trick, but now that we were back home, in the two times that we'd tried it, it hadn't worked.

I was irritated and horny, but that was nothing new so I got myself together and started my day.

"Patrice come over and sit with me, Micki isn't answering the phone.

"Oh, so I'm option number two?"

I laughed.

"Nope. Just come over. Eddie and the boys are gone and I'm bored."

"Well, I can't come. I'm about to go see a man about a *dog*."

Of course that was a saying that the old folks used that meant that she was going to have sex; which made me jealous as I replayed the whack ass sex that I'd just had with Eddie only about two hours ago.

"Well, I hope you don't like it," I teased.

"Oh? Are we talking about me or are we talking about you?" Patrice threw shade and with that she was gone.

Of course she and my other best friend Micki knew of my little problem, sexually, with my husband.

They were my voices of reason to keep going in spite of, well, Micki was anyway.

Patrice was a bitch.

At least seventy-five percent of the time.

I blamed that on the fact that she was an only child, a rich brat and didn't have any kids or a stable relationship.

The knock on the door stole my focus.

Polo.

He greeted me and walked right past me.

"I saw you in Hawaii," I said to Polo.

The trip had been about two weeks ago, but this was my first time seeing him.

Eddie had seen him a few times, but he hadn't been by the house, until now.

The distance wasn't normal.

He used to come by if not every day, every other day.

But for some reason he had been staying away.

"Yeah, so," he said and sat on our couch and starting flipping through the channels on the TV.

I rolled my eyes at him.

"So my butt Polo! Why didn't you say anything to us?"

"For what? The trip was for you guys to enjoy. I didn't need to say anything. You guys needed some alone time."

I stood at the entrance and just watched him.

I guess he was right, yet still it was strange that he'd decided to go at the same time that we did, and didn't bother to mention it to us or even speak to us.

"Y'all got something to drink?"

"It's too early for a drink Polo."

He smirked at me and got up from the couch and headed towards the kitchen.

I followed him.

I texted Eddie to let him know that he was there and waited for him to respond saying that he'd told him to come by and that he was only about five minutes away.

I watched Polo skim through the liquor cabinet before heading back into the living room.

He was going to drink himself to death.

Polo returned, with what looked like a glass of crown royal.

He sat back in his same spot on the couch across from me and took a sip of his drink.

"Why do you drink so much?"

Polo looked from side to side as though he didn't know who I was talking to.

"Where am I…therapy? I could have sworn that I was at my best friend's house and not at some bootleg counseling session," he replied sarcastically and took another sip.

"I was just asking. Seems like all you do is drink and have babies," I laughed and he did too.

"Well, at least I'm good at something. Never been good at much."

"Don't say that. Everyone has their talents. Yours just seem to revolve around booze, babies, oh and those sex toys."

"Ay, those sex toys made me millions," he said.

"Well, see, I guess that proves my point about you being good at something. Millions means that people really enjoy them obviously."

"Do you?"

"Do I what?"

"Do you enjoy them?"

What?

His question caught me by surprise.

I almost had to force myself to answer him.

"Uh, no," I said uncomfortably.

He could tell that his question had been inappropriate and he turned his attention towards the TV.

I had never tried any of his toys, but I'd heard great things about them from family and friends.

I figured that bringing toys into the bedroom with Eddie would probably make him cum even faster than he already did.

If that was even possible.

So, I didn't want to add anything else into the mix.

But maybe that was something that I could consider for myself though.

I already pleased myself from time to time with my fingers; I suppose a toy might make it a little easier.

There was an awkward silence between us as we both pretended to watch TV.

I immediately thought of the night of my husband's party.

Some of Polo's comments had been a little strange not to mention our little danced.

That had never happened before.

Something was definitely different with him.

We got along pretty good, for the most part, unless he did something stupid and Eddie was left to come to his rescue.

Other than that, we were okay.

But here lately, his approach towards me was odd.

Definitely out of the normal.

It was as though I was some kind of new girlfriend in his best friend's life that he was still trying to figure out if he liked or not.

I tried not to take it personal, but I'd noticed.

"So, there's this nice girl at my job that I think would be a perfect fit for you. I think you two should hook up. I told her that my husband had a friend that was single. She's wild, and a little crazy, but she also has that strong, independent woman side to her. I think you would like her. Can I give her your number?"

I was always trying to set Polo up with someone.

Hell, two of his baby's mamas were old co-workers of mine that I'd introduced him to.

But Polo was in his thirties as well and it was time for him to find a wife and settle down.

I mean, I would be lying to say that I didn't care about his well-being, because I did.

As close as he was with my husband and because he was always around, it would be good for him to have a wife that I could hang with.

I always felt like the third wheel, even though Eddie was *my* husband.

"No thank you. I'm good."

"Why not? She's a good fit for you."

"She ain't you," he mumbled.

He had been mumbling and saying a lot of things under his breath lately.

"What did you say Polo?"

"Nothing. I said that ain't nothing new. You always think you've found a good fit for me," he said.

That isn't what he'd said.

Or was I hearing things?

He didn't bother to give me eye contact and only a second later, the front door opened and in came Eddie and the kids.

Our sons were six and three and they meant the world to me. I loved them so much and I was willing to do anything to make sure that they were always happy.

They both headed in my direction and showered me with hugs and kisses.

Eddie followed behind them and leaned down to kiss me.

Out of the corner of my eye, I saw Polo glance in our direction but he quickly turned his attention back towards the TV.

Eddie headed towards him next.

Polo stood up.

"Hey bro," Eddie said and they did their little handshake and brotherly hug as usual.

They headed off to their man cave, and I was left to tend to the kids.

I know that I'd heard him correctly.

What did he mean that she wasn't me?

Of course she wasn't me.

I was sure that's what he'd said, but then again, maybe I was wrong.

I shook my head but the thoughts didn't go away.

Something was going on with Polo and I was going to make it my business to find out what it was.

"Has Polo been acting weird to you lately?" I asked my husband as we prepared for bed later on that night.

"Not really. His drinking is getting worse though."

"What do you think is behind it?"

"I don't know. Why? Has he said anything to you about it?"

I didn't know if I should mention the comment from earlier because now I was unsure if he'd even said it.

"No. I'd mentioned hooking him up again but---," I started to say, but Eddie cut me off.

"He doesn't like when you do that. He always says that he can find his own woman. Granted he usually ends up sleeping with them, but he complains that you were way off and that he was just doing something to pass time. Just leave him to his own match making okay? I think he needs to find one special lady and be done with it too, but he will when he's ready," Eddie signaled that the conversation was over and got in the bed beside of me.

He kissed me and I kissed him back.

I was hoping that he didn't want to fool around, but of course he did.

But for the first time, in a long time, I didn't get upset when he came just as fast as he always did.

I was actually glad that it was done and over with.

A few minutes after, Eddie was snoring, and I was left to lay there and dwell on my thoughts.

And for some reason or another, they were all about Polo.

.~***~

"Come on," I tugged at Eddie's shirt, leading him into the Women's bathroom.

Seeing that the coast was clear, we headed to the handicapped stall and I locked the door behind us.

"No Sassi, not here."

I kissed his neck.

We hadn't done anything spontaneous in years and I was trying to pull a few tricks out of the bag in hopes of making our sex life better.

I was trying to get that spark back.

I was trying to rekindle some flames.

Basically, I was trying to save my marriage.

"Stop Sassi. Someone just came in here," Eddie whispered.

"Shhh," I said to him and kissed him anyway.

He giggled and squirmed like a virgin and then he grabbed me by my wrists.

"No. Come on. Let's get out of here before someone sees us," he said, peeked out of the stall and seeing that the other woman was already using the bathroom, he scurried out of the stall like a little mouse and headed out the door.

Instead of following him, I stood there for a while.

Ugh!

Ole' punk ass!

I'm trying to help out or relationship, but he couldn't see that even if I wore a big ass sign with red letters that said "I'm Horny and Unhappy."

I'd been feeling really unhappy lately and though I'd done so well with hiding it and overlooking it before, it wasn't so easy all of a sudden.

But he just didn't get it.

Nevertheless, I took a deep breath, and headed out behind him.

Of course his boring ass was standing there waiting for me.

He looked at me and I didn't even try to hide my disappointment.

As we made our way back to the table, the waiter was standing there with our food.

We both smiled at her and sat down and started to eat.

"Do I make you happy Sassi?"

I looked at my husband.

Hell to the no, is what I wanted to say but I didn't.

With him actually asking the question, though I felt like I wasn't, I actually took the time to think it through.

It wasn't that he didn't make me happy, I was just unhappy with the way that our relationship had been lately.

The Hawaii trip had been the best time that we'd had together in a long time.

We just needed to get back to how we used to be.

Even back then I had small doubts and questions, but Eddie made it so that the issues that I saw didn't matter.

He made me forget the bad and simply enjoy the good.

I didn't need the whole flame; just a little spark would do.

If anything, I was unhappy that he didn't see it or feel it too.

But this might be the perfect opportunity to voice a few concerns, again.

But if I was going to do it, I had to do it just right.

So I lied.

"Of course. Why did you ask me that?"

"No reason. I just get the feeling that I'm not doing something right. I'm trying to be the best husband and father that I can be. I really am," Eddie said and took a bite of his food.

"And I really appreciate everything that you do I really do."

"I'm glad. Because I'm nothing without you. You know that right?

I nodded.

See, how in the hell was I supposed to complain about sex and the lack of excitement in our relationship now?

He was always so genuine, and so sweet, that it killed me to say anything that might hurt his feelings.

But he was just so damn boring!

And he needed to hear it.

We didn't really seem to have much in common these days, if we ever really did before.

If it wasn't about bills, sex, kids, or work, we didn't really have much to say to each other.

We told each other that we loved each other often, and he did crack a few jokes here and there, but that wasn't enough.

It just wasn't enough.

I needed more good sex and more good times with my husband.

If he could give me those two things, we would be fine.

I guess I should tackle the sex topic first.

"Oh you're so good to us. Thank you for being such a good husband and father. But I have to ask you this. Do you think that we are lacking some romance and fire? Does it feel like something is missing? Especially when it comes to chemistry and sex?"

I figured this was the best way to ease him into the conversation and my confessions.

"No. I think everything is fine. Don't you?"

Uh, hell no!

That was the purpose of me bringing it up, duh!

"Really?"

He couldn't be serious.

If he thought that, he wouldn't have tried a different approach with sex.

Eddie was far from a stupid man.

He sat his fork down.

No more saying it the nice way and being indirect, it was time to just put it all out there.

"Are you saying that I don't satisfy you Sassi?"

Here goes nothing.

"We've kind of had this conversation before. And with the way that you tried a different approach in Hawaii, I assumed that you noticed it too. I'm not saying that you don't satisfy me, I'm just saying that you don't bother to try to. Or maybe you want to but you can't. I'm not sure. I don't know just sometimes you finish really quickly; well, most of the time. And most times, I don't get anything out of it. So, I guess maybe I am what you would call not satisfied."

I took a deep breath.

There it is, in a nut shell.

I mean, he simply couldn't get mad at the truth.

"Okay."

I could tell that my comment either hurt his feelings or pissed him off but he just started eating again.

"No, let's talk about it."

"What is there to talk about? My wife doesn't like having sex with me."

"I didn't say that."

"You didn't have to."

"Don't be like this Eddie."

"Like what? I completely understand. My dick ain't good enough for you."

"I didn't say that. What I said was that you always get yours and I rarely get mine."

"Like I said, my dick ain't good enough."

"If that's how you want to take it Eddie, then fine. But that's not what I said. Yes, it has been better, and I'm just trying to find a solution."

"Or find a way out?"

And with that he got up, and walked away from the table.

We were at a restaurant so I asked for the check and a few minutes later, I headed out to find Eddie.

He had some what got offended the previous times that I'd tried to say it but never had he acted out like this.

I walked to the car and he was already in it with the engine running, waiting for me.

"Eddie," I said fastening my seat belt.

"You think I don't already know that my sex has changed. I do. Just hearing you say I don't please you makes it all realistic. I don't know what the problem is as I told you before."

Maybe he couldn't help it and I sort of felt bad that it was an issue, but was I supposed to do?

Deal with it forever?

"Sorry for the way I reacted. But no husband wants to hear that he doesn't sexually please his wife," Eddie said.

"It just goes by so fast. That's all that I was saying. Maybe it's stress from work."

"Maybe. But I'll fix it."

And with that, he started to drive.

For the most part I was just glad to have really gotten it off of my chest.

Maybe we could find ways to help him, together, and at least get our sex life back where it used to be.

Good sex would make everything else that I was feeling seem small and irrelevant.

Most of it anyway.

The excitement part of our relationship still needed to be discussed, but I would tackle that conversation another day.

There wasn't any point in adding fuel to a burning fire.

We picked up the kids from his parents, and once we were home and the kids were in bed, I felt bad, so making the first move, I came on to Eddie.

But he turned me down.

I was sure that his ego was a little bruised or maybe he wanted to wait until he figured out a solution to make it better.

Either way, I could understand, so I ran myself a bath and took care of myself.

I liked it better when I did it anyway.

~***~

Things around the house were still a little tensed but I could tell that Eddie was concerned and thinking of a way to make me happy.

That's just the type of man that he was.

He hadn't even attempted to touch me and I had found the time to tell him that we didn't have any fun anymore and that we needed to do something spontaneous from time to time.

The look on his face when I told him said it all.

"If this bitch complain about one more damn thing!"

He didn't say it, but I knew that he had to be thinking it.

But I was just trying to get our marriage back in a better place; a happy place or at least a place where I could forget all of the obvious and just focus on the positives.

"Where's Eddie?"

"I don't know. He said that he would be back soon."

Polo seemed nervous.

"I need to talk to him."

"Call him."

"No. I need to do it face to face. I'll wait."

"Well, I'm a good listener. I might can help," I offered my services and sat beside Polo in a rocking chair on the front porch.

"No. It's guy stuff."

"Oh."

I pondered the thought of mentioning what was going on with me and Eddie.

If Eddie was going to listen to anybody, it was going to be Polo.

Polo could get things through him that I couldn't.

I was sure of it.

Maybe I could be limited with details but tell him enough to get results.

My biggest concern was whether or not Polo would mention our conversation to Eddie. If Eddie found out that I'd discussed private, intimate matters with Polo, he would surely die.

Or maybe I would come up missing or something.

Either way, he would be pissed!

"Well, I have a favor to ask of you."

"Anything."

"Well, it's kind of personal."

"About you?"

"And Eddie."

"What? You wouldn't want me to say anything to him about the conversation?"

"I do. But I don't. It's complicated."

"What is it?"

"If I tell you, you can't tell him that I told you. But maybe you could discuss the topic or something."

"What is it?"

"Well, we have been having some trouble lately."

"Sex trouble?"

"He told you?"

"We tell each other everything."

Well, of course they did.

"So what did you tell him to do?"

"I have a few ideas. That's actually what I was coming to talk to him about."

I looked at him with relief.

Leave it to Polo to have a solution.

"Don't worry. Y'all will be humping like rabbits from now on."

The way he said it made me uneasy.

"Is whatever it is safe?"

"Yeah. I haven't tried it because I don't need it, but I've heard great things."

My mind was about to go left, but I didn't allow it to.

"Well, thanks."

"No thanks needed. I'll do anything for him, especially if it involves saving his marriage. Even if it isn't easy," he said.

"What does that mean?"

Eddie pulled up and Polo smiled.

"Like I said, even if it isn't easy."

He left me sitting on the porch and headed to meet Eddie before he was even out of the car.

Even if what isn't easy?

Was Polo jealous of our marriage?

I left them to chat, and I headed in the house with hope in my heart.

I hope whatever Polo had up his sleeve actually works for Eddie and I.

And that was nothing but the truth.

~***~

So…things were better!

Thanks to Polo!

I wasn't sure what kind of pill Eddie had gotten from him or where Polo had told him to go and get it, but he had recently been a beast in the bedroom and it was me that couldn't keep up these days.

The sex was lasting almost *too* long sometimes and I would be the one to tap out or at least need a day in between to recover from the *pound* game that Eddie would put on me.

The good news was that now I was always satisfied first; but Eddie had to damn near kill himself to get his.

He would pump and pump and it would seem like he was constipated with at nut or something.

I could tell by the look on his face sometimes that it was bothersome and just when he would be about to say forget it, he got *it*.

But I could tell that he didn't care about anything except for making me happy.

And sexually, finally, I was.

As far as putting a lot more fun back into our relationship, it wasn't happening yet.

I could tell that on some days he would try to pretend to be someone that he wasn't to keep me smiling and laughing, and enjoying his presence.

But I could see straight through it.

I couldn't change who he was or who he had become.

He could only pretend for so long and then he would go right back to being himself.

And I had to set my feelings aside and realize that he was who he was and he had been the same man since before we were married.

I accepted it then.

So I had to deal with it now.

I couldn't change him, nor could Polo's talks change him.

But I could manage.

Hell, I had been for years.

"Take out enough to cook for Polo too. He's coming over tonight," Eddie said on the phone.

I was already home from work and enjoying my two hours to myself before Eddie was off and picked up the kids to come home.

Hanging up, I headed to the kitchen and pulled out enough steak for my family, and Polo, poured myself a cup of iced tea and headed back to the living room to relax.

I thought to make a few phone calls and girl talk, but I decided against that.

I didn't want to do anything.

Just for a little while I wanted to enjoy doing nothing.

I thought about my life and where I really wanted to be professionally.

It was about time that I found my dream job; writing somewhere, anywhere.

The book writing idea had been on my mind so heavy lately and maybe it was time to do something about it.

I never seemed to have time to do anything for myself or anything that I actually enjoyed.

And then it hit me.

These two hours alone, five days a week could come in handy.

I had a brand new lap top that I hardly ever used.

It had been a gift from Polo.

Of course, he and Eddie knew of my love for writing and last year he'd gotten me the most expensive lap top that he could find as a Christmas present.

A little too much, but Eddie said to simply accept it, stating that Polo had the money to waste, and that it wasn't a big deal.

Polo had always said that I would make a good writer because I talked too much, and because I always had an opinion.

I chuckled at how right he was.

From being lost in my thoughts, my two hours of alone time seemed more like ten minutes because soon, Eddie and the kids were walking through the front door.

"I missed you."

"I believe you," I chimed flirtatiously to Eddie.

Shortly after, Polo arrived and the rest of the night went by with a breeze.

We ate, laughed, reminisced and managed to have a very good time, which we always did if Polo was there.

The guys had a few drinks and once the kids were off to bed, we continued our conversations about the past.

They talked about childhood memories, and of course old girlfriends and women.

I could tell by the look on Polo's face that things were about to go left.

And I was right.

"You were supposed to be mine," Polo said aloud.

I stared at him, and then looked at Eddie who shrugged his shoulders.

"Go on, tell her Eddie. Tell her what you did," Polo slurred.

He was about two drinks past drunk and from the way that Eddie giggled he wasn't too far behind him.

"Shut up," Eddie laughed but I wanted to know what Polo was talking about.

"He stole you from me."

Eddie chuckled and took Polo's drink.

But Polo picked up the bottle instead.

"Tell her how you stole her."

"I didn't steal her. How can I steal something you never had?"

Okay, so what were they talking about?

I was confused.

"What is he talking about Eddie?"

"Oh, nothing baby. He's just talking about that night at the bar."

"Damn right. I noticed you first. I had been looking at you all night and he knew it too. And soon as I took my eye off of him, bam, he was over there sweet talking you or whatever it is that he wanted to call it. Next thing I know, y'all a couple and shit," Polo proclaimed.

I giggled at the looks on both of their faces at Polo's comments, but I was definitely thinking about his statement.

What?

I never knew that.

How come Eddie never told me that before?

"You snooze. You lose my brother," Eddie said and they jumped to another subject.

I found it funny that Polo had been interested in me.

I couldn't imagine being with someone like him, but then again, like I said, other than his few bad habits, he wasn't all that bad.

He definitely had the sense of humor and the charm, but Polo was a little too friendly with his penis for my liking.

And as far as I knew, he always had been.

I listened to them cackle for another hour or so and seeing that they were both wasted, Eddie offered Polo the couch but instead he wanted to go home.

So, Eddie asked me to take him.

After making sure that Eddie was fine, I helped Polo out the door and to my car.

He was leaving his car at our house until morning.

I drove slowly, hoping that Polo didn't become nauseous.

"Polo do you need some air?" I asked him.

"No. I'm not drunk," he said clearly.

He wasn't talking all slurred like he had been only moments before.

He wasn't looking at me, instead he looked straight ahead.

"What do you mean that you're not drunk?"

"Like I said, I'm not drunk. Tipsy, definitely. But I'm not drunk. Not at all."

"But you were just drunk a few minutes ago."

"No I wasn't. I was never drunk Sassi."

I looked at him briefly and then back at the road.

Then why had he pretended to be?

He just got weirder and weirder every single day.

"So, you were pretending to be drunk?"

"I guess."

"Why?"

He didn't answer my question.

Instead, he started talking about something else.

"That night at the bar wasn't the first time that I saw you. I'd seen you a few times before then. I'd always said that I was going to get up the nerve to talk to you. Just looking at you I could tell that you were different and that when I stepped to you, I had to step correct," Polo said clearly.

What?

"I told Eddie that night that you were the girl that I had told him about. The girl that I had been afraid to talk to and I have never been afraid to talk to any woman, ever, except for you. It was just something about you. Something about the way you walked and the way you moved. Once, I'd seen you at a gas station and I followed you, just to see where you would go or what you would do next. Just to try to figure you out."

Ole' stalking ass!

Strangely, I'd never seen Polo before that night at the bar. He and Eddie were a few years older than I was and I figured that was why I hadn't seen either of them around prior to that night.

"I saw you walk into the bar that night. It was fate. I just knew that it was fate. I talked about you all night. I kept saying that I was going to make my move but I just needed a few drinks to loosen me up. But after a few drinks, I was in full party mode and my attention was on having a good time. But Eddie knew. He knew that I wanted you. He knew how beautiful you were to me and how scared I had been to approach you. I guess maybe he saw it in you too and strangely he was bold enough to make a move. Even that was a surprise to me."

I was quiet and I tried to get my thoughts together.

I mean, even if Polo had approached me that night, I doubted that I would have been interested.

He was a player; a ladies man.

He was the type of man that I had been running from back then.

Physically, he was attractive; but there was nothing sexy about a man who boned more women a year than most men did in a lifetime.

STD's are real and I didn't want any parts of all of that.

"Why are you telling me this now?"

"I don't know. Hell, in the beginning you were pretty much dating me *and* him anyway."

"What? What do you mean?"

"I mean after he told me that you guys exchanged numbers, I had no choice but to get over it and see it for what it was. But you know Eddie. You know how he is and he just didn't think that he had what it takes to make you really want him. He didn't think that he had the right personality to make you love him. So, he asked for my help."

You mean to tell me that I had been bamboozled?

Well I'll be damned!

"I was the one telling him what to say to you. I would be right in front of him, telling him what to say and how to say it. Almost every phone conversation that you had in the beginning, I was around him. Sitting right next to him. Coaching him through it."

"Stop lying Polo."

"I'm not lying."

I was sure that he wasn't.

That was the sad thing.

"I told him what to wear when he took you out. I told him where to take you and why to take you there. Hell I taught him to pay attention to your body language and when to make the right moves. I did that because he was my friend. I did that because I could see that he really wanted the chance to know you and love you. I did it despite what I felt. And it worked. He hooked you like a fish and you ended up marrying him."

What kind of mess was this?

Did I feel some kind of way?

Hell yeah, I did.

I mean, it did explain as to why Eddie was a completely different man today than he had been in the very beginning.

I guess he was being the man that Polo had told him to be instead of being himself.

I could only assume that once he proposed and I said yes, that he no longer needed Polo's assistance and he probably didn't feel the need to have to try so hard anymore.

Now that I was thinking about it, it wasn't until after he proposed that I really started to feel small feelings that he may not be "the one".

Eddie was a lot of things, good things, but I knew that what Polo was saying was true.

I guess Polo had just helped make him appealing.

And he had done just that.

I felt deceived.

I even felt a little tricked into loving Eddie but what did Polo want me to do with it?

Why was he telling me all of this now?

"Well, that's the past. What do you want? A thank you?"

Polo chuckled.

"No. I want you."

Here we go with this again mess!

And this time I'd heard him loud and clear.

"I loved you first."

"No you didn't."

"Yes I did."

"You didn't even know me."

"Doesn't mean that I didn't love you."

"Polo, you can't say stuff like that. And we both know that that's really inappropriate to say don't you think?"

"I'm drunk. I don't know what I'm saying."

"I thought you just said that you weren't drunk?"

"And you believed me?"

What?

We pulled up at his house and he didn't hesitate to get out of the car.

He walked slowly, and I couldn't help but ask him one last question.

I just had to ask.

"Polo?"

He turned around.

"Do you wish that you had said something to me? That night? Or the times that you'd seen me before?"

I didn't really know why I wanted to know the answer to that question, but I did.

And I knew that he was going to answer it.

"Every day. Every single day," he said and he walked away.

I drove off speechless.

Polo used to have a thing for me?

And from the looks of it, maybe he still did.

Or maybe he didn't.

I was confused.

I debated whether I should inform Eddie of our little discussion.

I was sure that Polo wasn't supposed to say anything and it made sense as to why Eddie brushed off the topic at dinner.

To be honest, if Eddie had been himself completely, from the very beginning, I was sure that I would have married him.

He was smart, kind, loving, genuine and all of that good stuff, but he wasn't quite right for me.

We weren't a perfect fit.

But they didn't make men these days like Eddie and I wasn't giving him up.

No other woman was going to get him.

Unless I was dead.

But it does make me wonder.

If Polo had told Eddie what to say and what to do in order to get me and keep me, then who had I really fallen in love with?

Was it Eddie?

Or was it an imitation of Polo?

Polo had definitely dropped one hell of a bomb on me and my heart and mind felt as though they were both about to explode.

I would have preferred for him to have kept that secret between him and Eddie.

But it was out now.

And still there wasn't a thing that I could do with it.

At the end of the day, I was married to Eddie.

And at that moment, it was clearer than ever.

I wasn't going to give him up despite the issues that I knew that I could find a way to deal with.

I loved my boring, workaholic, no fun, only good sex with a pill, husband.

Eddie was mine and I was keeping him.

Damn right, I was keeping him.

Most of the men in the world were just like Polo, except for Eddie, and I had him all to myself.

I would be a fool to let him go.

I turned up the radio, shook away my thoughts and I headed home to *my* husband.

Eddie and I were in this thing until death and I wasn't giving him up for Polo or anyone else.

Period.

****

CHAPTER 3

"Hello?"

"Don't say anything. Just listen. I was just thinking about you. I just needed to hear your voice. I can't seem to get you out of my mind, no matter how hard I try. It's wrong, but it feels so right. If only you were mine…bye."

Polo hung up.

"Who was that honey?"

"I don't know. Private call again. They didn't say anything. They just hung up." I lied.

Why was I lying to Eddie?

I wasn't sure.

Well, yes I was.

There was no way in hell that I could tell Eddie that it was Polo and tell him what he'd said.

Ever since Polo's little car ride confession, his behavior towards me had changed yet again.

This time it was in a flirty, obsessive kind of way.

He was becoming more and more inappropriate with me, every day, and he even getting a little touchy feely whenever he could do it without being noticeable.

I would fuss and curse at him, but he found it amusing.

But I knew that it was only an amount of time before Eddie caught his ass.

So I decided that it was time to tell my husband.

Well, kind of.

"Why didn't you tell me that Polo helped you snag me?"

I tried to sound as though the conversation wasn't about to turn serious, but it was.

Eddie snickered.

"He told you that?"

"You both did the other night when you were drinking."

"No, he said I stole you from him. He didn't say anything about helping me "snag you" as you called it."

"Yes he did. On the way home he continued with his drunken spat and he mentioned assisting you when it came to dating me. We both know that a drunken man tells no tales so what's up with that huh?"

"So he gave me a few pointers, so what? I felt that you were a little out of my league. I was so nervous around you and I wanted to make a good impression. So, sure, after he got over the fact that we'd hit it off, I'd asked him for a little advice. Nothing big. Nothing serious. He's a ladies man, we both know that. So, who better to get advice from when it came to wanting to impress a beautiful lady?"

He said it like it wasn't a big deal.

I guess it wasn't all that bad once he'd put it that way.

"Well, since that night, Polo seems to be a little different towards me. Maybe it's nothing but he has definitely been strange."

Eddie simply nodded.

"I'll talk to him."

I opened my mouth to say something else, but Eddie was done with the conversation.

I didn't get the chance to give him any details because he walked away.

I was sure that he was going to mention it to Polo but I was also sure that Polo was going to act like he didn't know what he was talking about.

But, hey, at least I'd tried.

I'd done my part.

That was all that mattered.

Besides, Polo was nothing to worry about.

I was sure of it.

It was Saturday and as Eddie headed to play basketball with Polo and a few of his other friends, I decided to take the kids to the park with one of my best friend's Micki.

Micki was as crazy as they came and I do mean crazy.

But I loved her to death.

She was that ghetto fabulous friend that was loud and embarrassing half of the time, but you loved her and kept her around because she was extremely loyal and she knew way too much about you and your past.

She knew all of my dirty little secrets and some of them could hurt and destroy some of the people that I loved the most.

So she was stuck being my friend forever.

It had been a while, and it was time for us to catch up.

Patrice was supposed to have met us there, but she changed her mind saying that she wasn't in the mood to be around a lot of kids.

I'd actually been friends with Patrice first, and then she introduced me to Micki and all three of us have been so close ever since.

I loved those women unconditionally, and had it not been for them, I would have given up on my marriage and everything else a long time ago.

With the kids dressed, we headed out the door but just as we were backing out, Polo pulled into the driveway behind me.

I sat looking at him from the rearview mirror and soon he got out of his Jag to approach my car.

"Where is Eddie?"

"He went to meet you at the court."

"He told me to pick him up."

"I guess he forgot. He drove."

Polo nodded and spoke to the kids and then he looked at me.

"You look beautiful today as always Sassi," he whispered.

He was absolutely flirting with me…again!

And I didn't know how to feel about it.

He was my husband's best friend, but he wasn't acting like it.

"Look Polo, I don't know what has gotten into you lately, but I love Eddie okay?"

"I love him too."

"You're not acting like it. He's your best friend, you know."

"I know that."

"Then stop coming on to his wife."

"I'm coming on to the woman that was supposed to be *my* wife. You fell in love with me, not him. You're just to blind to see that. But fine. Okay."

And with that, he headed back to his car and drove away.

I turned a movie on the car DVD for the kids to keep them quiet so that I could sit and get my thoughts together for a second.

Polo was crazy.

He was absolutely insane.

I couldn't believe the things that he actually let come out of his mouth.

I was not supposed to be *his* wife.

Where in the hell was he getting that from?

Sure, he had been behind Eddie's actions, and comments in the beginning, but I never would have chosen him over Eddie.

Right?

No, I'm sure that I wouldn't have.

I mean, was he attractive?

Sure.

He didn't look better than Eddie though, but he did have a sort of swag about him that would make a woman notice him before they would notice my husband.

My husband was simple.

Even when he wore his suits, they were always pretty simple.

He was basic.

Normal.

But Polo was a different story.

He always looked good in whatever he wore and he wasn't afraid to make the style his own or play around with colors.

He definitely caught your eye that was for sure.

And if the way that he looked didn't make you notice him, his personality would.

He was funny.

Very witty and used his vocabulary in a way that I'd seen blow the minds of every woman that he had a conversation with.

I'd watched him weave his web of deceit time and time again and women fell for it every single time.

But that's just who he was.

A womanizer.

Nothing more. Nothing less.

I pulled off and drove like a bat out of hell and headed to the park.

I couldn't wait to talk to Micki.

"Hey girl," she said at the sight of me and we both smiled at the kids as all five of them ran towards the playground.

Micki had three kids and one of which was my nephew.

Though we were friends first, she used to date my little brother and although things didn't work out between them, we'd still remained the best of friends.

"So what's been going on with you lately?"

"Same ole, same ole. What about you? Is Eddie hitting that thing like he used to yet?" Micki laughed.

As I said, we told each other everything.

"Actually, things couldn't be better with Eddie and I. We are fine but—," I started to say and Micki waited for me to finish.

"Polo has been flirting with me," I confessed to her.

"Well, it's about damn time," she replied.

I looked at her confused.

"Girl don't play. Chile, I peeped it a long time ago. He's had a thing for you for years. I could see it in his eyes when he looked at you. I could see how his body tensed up if you got too close to him as though he was scared to inhale the scent of your skin out of fear of wanting to jump your bones or something. It's always been obvious to me. The only people that couldn't see it were you and Eddie," Micki said.

I tried to think back to the previous years to see if there was any truth to what she was saying, but I just couldn't see it.

Polo had never done anything to indicate that he had some kind of *thing* for me until recently.

We'd been alone plenty of times and he was always around, but never had he made a pass at me or seemed uncomfortable by my presence.

"At one point I thought that maybe you guys had some kind of affair or something going on and he was just whipped by the booty, but I figured that you would have told me if you guys had sex or something. So now he's making it clear Sassi?"

"Crystal."

"Well, what are you going to do about it? Have you told Eddie?"

"Yeah, well, no. I mean, I mentioned it and he said that he was going to talk to Polo."

"Well what I want to know is would you?"

"Would I what?"

"Would you *do* Polo?"

I looked at her and rolled my eyes.

"What? I can't answer that Micki."

"Sure you can. Would you do Polo? You gotta' give it to him, not only is he fine, but we've heard about how good he is in bed. So, if you weren't with Eddie, would you do him?"

I thought about her question, and I was disappointed by my answer, so I kept it to myself.

"I plead the fifth," I giggled.

"Um huh, I bet you do."

~***~

"Excuse me," Polo said touching the small of my back.

"Really Polo? Stop it."

" What? I said excuse me," he said, reaching for the bottle of wine on the counter.

He lingered for a second too long, breathing on my neck and my left ear.

He chuckled softly.

"You have no idea what I would do to you," he said softly.

"Not a damn thing. And if you keep it up, I'm going to tell Eddie."

"Go ahead. Who do you think he's going to believe? Me or you?"

Hell, he had a point there.

"Just stop okay."

"For now. But one of these days…"

And then headed back out of the kitchen.

I stood at the sink and internally scowled myself.

Why did I have goosebumps?

Why did I have butterflies in the pit of my belly?

It was as though a surge of energy had shot from my chest, rolled around in my belly and then thumped me on my throbbing clit.

I wasn't aroused, but I was something.

Maybe it was because Eddie and I hadn't had sex in a while.

He'd stopped taking the pills because he'd said that they were giving him headaches.

He also said that another side effect of them was that days after taking one it would be hard for him to pee.

But he wouldn't even think about touching me without them, or let me touch him.

I'd tried, but he would refuse.

I told him to try it without one of them, just once.

Maybe the pills had his stamina back where it needed to be and he might even discover that he no longer needed any assistance.

But he wouldn't do it no matter how much I begged.

He just said that he would take one of the pills soon and asked if I could wait until then for sex.

I really wondered if Eddie would believe Polo over me.

I was his wife, but Polo was his best friend.

I truly didn't know if he would take my word over his.

That alone was a sad case all in itself.

"Whoo!" I jumped at his touch.

"What's wrong baby? I scared you?" Eddie said.

"A little. I was daydreaming."

"Oh really? About what?"

"You."

At least it wasn't a lie.

Eddie smiled.

"What's wrong?"

"Nothing. I just wanted to tell you that I loved you."

"I love you too."

"How much?"

"More than you will ever know."

That was the realest thing I'd said in a long time.

I did love him and the love that I had for him is what gave me the strength to keep pressing on.

"Are you going to be tired later? Or do you want me to pop a pill in a few?" Eddie whispered in my ear and then licked it.

Tickled, I nodded my head yes.

Those pills had given him a little boost of confidence too and regularly he was being all nasty and stuff.

He was finally becoming a little more comfortable with admitting that he needed the assistance.

At first he wouldn't even say the word "pill".

He was only in his thirties, so I was sure that it bothered him but it was what it was.

Maybe one day he would get his mojo back and if he didn't, thank heavens for modern medicine.

"Ugh, get a room," Polo said, walking in and looking in the cabinet for more alcohol.

Eddie immediately moved away from me and started talking to him.

"You don't need anything else to drink because you need to be able to drive home," I said to Polo with condemning eyes.

He sat the bottle down on the counter.

"You're right. I need to get ready to go anyway."

He sat his glass down beside it and then he and Eddie high fived.

"Why do you drink so much anyway?" Eddie quizzed him.

"That's what people do when they're unhappy. They drink."

And with that he reached walked over and gave me a pound and patted Eddie on the shoulder.

Eddie walked him to the door and when he returned to the kitchen, he smiled.

"I'm going to take the pill and run you a bath. I'll see you when you get done," he said and headed to our bedroom.

I finished the dishes and finished straightening up the kitchen and once I was all done, I picked up my phone from the table.

I had two messages, so I checked them.

Both were from Polo.

"I drink because I'm unhappy. I'm unhappy because I can't have you."

That was his first message.

The second message said:

"Erase these messages."

And just as he'd suggested, I erased them.

Oh hell…

What was I getting myself into?

~***~

"Are you writing again?" Eddie asked.

I had been finding anytime that I could to start writing.

I'd even managed to apply for a few writing jobs, but since I hadn't heard anything yet, I was working hard at trying to write a book.

Things were moving slowly, but day by day, I was finding new things to write about and it seemed as though everywhere I turned, I found some type of inspiration.

"Yes, only for a little while longer."

"No, come on baby. You said that a little while ago."

"I know, I'm just really into it."

"For what? It ain't like you don't already have a real job. Writing that little book is getting all of our quality time. Hubby before hobby baby. Hubby before hobby."

For some reason, Eddie's words stung my heart like a thousand bees.

This little book?

Hubby before hobby?

I knew that he wasn't intentionally trying to be mean but at the moment he did sound unsupportive as hell.

I'd been telling him for years that writing was where my heart is but I guess he had said how he really felt about it.

But I closed the laptop and headed to give him the time that he'd asked for.

Our relationship was in a decent place and there wasn't any reason to start an argument.

The kids were already asleep so for the next two hours I cuddled with Eddie.

I pretended to watch the movie with him until he fell asleep.

As soon as I heard him snore, I slid out of bed and headed back into the living room.

But I'd be damned if I didn't get one hell of a surprise.

Polo was sitting there.

"What the hell are you doing here?"

"I used my spare key to get in."

"That's not what I asked you. I asked you what you were doing here," I said with an attitude.

Of course he had a key to our place and we had one to his; though we hardly ever went over there because he always came to us.

I was surprised that I hadn't even heard him come in, nor had he called to say that he was coming.

Polo just looked at me and didn't respond.

I couldn't tell if he was drunk or not, but I was sure that he probably was.

"Eddie is asleep so you can let yourself out," I said to him and headed to the desk but discovered that my laptop wasn't there.

"I got dropped off over here. It's closer than my house and I didn't want this new chick that I'm seeing to know where I lived. I'd been drinking at the restaurant and she wouldn't let me drive myself. So, I had her bring me here."

I didn't give him any eye contact.

Actually, I was still looking for my laptop.

"Oh, it's right here," he said.

I looked at him to see that my laptop was beside him.

"I read it. It's amazing. I can't wait until you're done. I always knew that you would make a great writer," he praised me and I walked over to him.

Hearing him say those words made my heart smile.

"Really Polo?"

"Yeah, you're gonna be great at this writing thing. I always knew it. So, here, write your heart out," he said handing me the laptop.

"Thank you."

He nodded.

"I've always wondered when you were going to go for it. I can't wait to see the finished product. Or see you name on a best-sellers list. I want an autographed copy."

"Sure."

Wow.

Even Polo was more supportive than Eddie.

Now that through me for a loop.

We chatted about writing for a little while longer.

"So is it cool if I crash on the couch?"

He asked taking off his shoes and stretching out before I even answered.

I didn't even respond.

I simply headed to get him a blanket.

I reached it towards him and just as he took it he touched my hand.

What was this that I was feeling?

"Thank you."

His hand touched mine for a second longer and then he took the blanket, covered himself up, and turned his back to me.

"Polo, nothing can happen between us."

Without turning back around to face me, he responded.

"If you say so."

Taking the laptop with me, I placed it on the dresser, glanced at Eddie and then headed to the bathroom.

I locked the bathroom door, turned on the shower, and then laid on the bathroom floor.

Finding my *spot*, I touched myself like never before, but for the first time I didn't imagine as though I was having really good sex with my husband.

I imagined that I was having sex with Polo instead.

~***~

"When will you be coming back home?"

"Well, I was going to come before heading to France to visit my father. But he decided that we should meet up in Paris, since that was where I was heading next. He and his new wife wanted to go there too," Patrice said with disgust.

She hated the fact that her father remarried, but he deserved to live out the rest of his days with someone, in love, in my opinion.

"Oh. Well, I miss you."

"Miss you too."

"I have so much to tell you."

"About Polo? Micki beat you to it. I talked to her the other day and she told me."

"Dang. Can I at least share my own problem?"

Micki always had talked too much.

"I don't like Polo. I never have. So, I say stay away from him."

"You don't like him because he is a male version of you."

"No. I just don't like him. Something about him."

"You barely like Eddie."

"I like him more than Polo."

She always said that. Personally, I thought that secretly she'd always hoped that Polo showed her some kind of interest, but he hadn't.

"Well, if you decide to give him the booty, I hope it's even worse than having sex with Eddie," Patrice said.

I didn't bother to tell her that Eddie and I had been having good sex lately.

She would just find something negative to say about that too.

We conversed for a few more seconds and then we got off of the phone.

I was about to go on my lunch break, and a small girl wearing a hat and carrying balloons and flowers came in.

I smiled thinking that they were from Eddie, but reading the card, they were from Polo.

"Just something to make you smile."

And they had done just yet.

This was definitely not appropriate, but I found myself smiling anyway.

"Nice flowers."

I looked up to see Eddie.

What was he doing here?

"I came to take you to lunch. Who are the flowers from?"

I had to think of a lie fast so I said that my boss had given them to me as a thank you for all of my hard work.

I wasn't sure if Eddie bought the story or not, but he didn't say anything.

I balled up the small card from Polo and dropped it in the trash can.

Yikes!

That could have gone a lot different…

~***~

"Hey."

I was so uncomfortable.

"Hey."

"Can I tell you something?"

I looked at Polo.

It seemed as though every time he opened his mouth nonsense fell out of it.

"I can't stop thinking about you."

He was on my mind, a lot, lately, and not in a friendly way; in a nasty, freaky way.

I was so ashamed.

I felt so bad and dirty and it was hard for me to keep it all together.

I found myself asking why did he have to be my husband's best friend?

And because he'd helped Eddie trick me into loving him, was my reality that I should have really married my husband's best friend instead?

I looked at Polo as he headed back over to sit down beside my husband.

It was Easter, and all of our family and friends were here.

I watched Polo as he talked and as he sipped from his glass.

I was definitely seeing him in a different light and I hated it.

I hated feeling some kind of way about him that I knew that I wasn't supposed to feel.

Polo and I were sneaking and texting, all day, every day.

Eddie was too busy most of the time to even noticed.

And it seemed as though every day Polo was surprising me with some of the things that he said and some of his thoughts.

He showered me with encouragement and every day that we texted for hours on end, we seemed to grow closer and closer.

And I was terrified of what could possibly be the outcome.

Shaking it off, I headed to join them.

I sat beside Eddie's mother as she talked.

For the most part, Eddie's mother and I had never had a problem.

She was quite fond of me and I'll admit, she was a pretty good mother-in-law too.

"Hey darling, so Eddie tells me that you have been writing lately," she said.

"Yep and I wish she would stop."

I looked at Eddie with hatred in my eyes.

"All she do is write. Half of the time I have to remind her that she has a husband and kids. That laptop is getting all of her time and attention. I blame you for buying that thing Polo," Eddie said.

Ugh, his lack of support with my writing was really starting get on my nerves.

Bastard!

He was always saying something slick and it bothered me that he wasn't as supportive about it like I'd thought that he would be.

He was nowhere near as supportive as Polo.

It just wasn't like him to act this way about something that I loved or something that was important to me.

Maybe another side effect to those penis pills was jackass syndrome, because that was exactly what he'd been acting like lately.

"Shut up Eddie. Have you even read what she's working on? It's good," Polo stood up for me.

"Oh and you have?"

"Yep. I read some of it. She might be the next best-selling author. You just never know."

Eddie looked at Polo and then looked at me.

His mind was racing, I could see it all over his face, but he didn't say anything else negative.

"Hmm, maybe I will read it then. You're right. I just never know," he finally said.

Luckily, my mother walked in and I headed away from the tension, to meet her at the door.

My mother, Mrs. Darlene Sampson, was the best mother in the world!

She'd done a fabulous job raising me and my younger brother.

And with a Daddy like mine, that wasn't easy.

He was dead and gone now, but he'd died doing the one thing that he loved more than his wife and kids…

Drinking.

He was nothing but a drunk and always had been.

In a way, Polo reminded me of him; and that was another reason why Polo wouldn't have had a chance from the start.

Daddy worked and paid the bills, but his drinking was way out of control, and no one hated his drunken ways more than me.

He disgusted me and I hated the ground that he walked on.

He was so non-existent that most of the time I forgot that he was even around.

I hadn't even allowed him to come to my wedding nor did I ever let him around my children.

I didn't trust him, especially after Patrice accused him of touching her.

She'd stayed over one weekend and she'd said that Daddy had come into the bathroom that Sunday morning, after she'd just gotten out of the shower and she said that he touched her.

I wasn't sure whether to call it molestation or inappropriately fondling or what, but either way, it was sick!

Patrice said that Daddy was drunk, early as usual, and said that he'd burst into the bathroom, noticed her naked body and then made his move on her.

Patrice accused Daddy of touching her *teenage kitty* and somewhat hunching her up against the wall, as she described it.

She'd come into my bedroom like a zombie and I knew immediately that something was wrong.

She told me and said that she wouldn't tell authorities because she loved me and didn't want to take my daddy away from me, although I told her to get his ass put in jail.

But she didn't say a word except that she would never spend the night again or be in the same house as him, and she never did.

I'd told Mama and she believed that he'd done it too.

But she never left his side.

She never made excuses for him, yet she stayed with him until his dying day.

She used to say all the time that she couldn't wait for him to drop dead, and one day, she'd gotten her wish.

He was talking to her and right in the middle of his sentence he clutched his chest and fell to the floor.

Dead.

And today, without Daddy, she was happier than I'd ever seen her before.

I'd always said that I wouldn't marry a drunk and that I didn't want a man who couldn't handle his liquor.

Eddie was that man.

He wasn't the heaviest drinker and he only drank if he was at home and with Polo; or if for some reason he talked me into having a few drinks with him.

But seriously, it was as though we kept liquor in the house, just for Polo.

Thinking about it now, Polo seemed to be going down the same path as Daddy, which reminded me that the little feelings that I had been feeling towards Polo lately were nonsense.

"Hey mommy," I smiled and hugged her.

"How you been baby?" She asked, following me to the kitchen.

"I've been good. Everything is fine. I've been writing, so I'm excited about that," I said to her.

"Good. Finally."

"Yeah, finally. But Eddie doesn't seem to like it. He's not as supportive of it, not like I thought that he would be. Polo is more supportive with it than he his."

"Polo?" Mama asked as though she was unsure as to why I'd even mentioned him.

Why had I mentioned him?

My mother stared at me and then she placed her hands on her hips.

"Is there something going on with you and Polo, Sassi?"

"What? No. He's Eddie's best friend, Ma," I said and headed towards the back door.

She followed me.

"Don't mess up your good marriage for some horny drunk chile. You saw what I went through with your father. And yes, he is Eddie's best friend. I didn't raise a slut," she warned.

"Okay Ma. But nothing is going on between us. He's like a brother to me."

I could tell that she wasn't convinced but she let the conversation go and started a new one.

I exhaled.

I had to get myself together.

I definitely shouldn't have said that.

She talked about something random, but shortly after, she made her way back to Eddie and I.

"Eddie will come around. He loves you so much Sassi," Mama said and then I heard her as she left the kitchen.

Yeah, I'm sure that he would.

But when?

I stepped outside to get some fresh air.

I headed to hide behind the outhouse so that no one could see me and I took a seat on the ground.

It was hotter than usual for Easter Sunday, but I was enjoying the weather and the warm rays from the sun against my skin.

I loved the springtime.

I loved the beauty of the blooming flowers and even the sound of the birds returning from the far south from the winter.

"Want some company?"

Polo scared the crap out of me.

How did he know that I was hiding behind here?

Before I could answer him, he sat down.

"Polo, just go away."

"No."

"Why?"

"Because you don't want me to."

Liar!

I did.

Kind of.

He scooted close to me and though I wanted to put some space in between us, I didn't.

"Polo," I started to say.

"Don't talk. Just listen. I don't want to feel this way about you either, but I do. For years I tried to fight it or find someone that had all of the things that I liked about you but none of them were you. Why do you think I deal with so many women? Granted I loved women before, but the past few years I've been searching for an imitation of you. I've been searching for your replacement Sassi. But I can't find her. I can't find her because there is no other you," he said.

My stomach was boiling and I felt as though I was about to be sick.

This could not be happening to me.

This had to be some kind of joke or dream that I was going to wake up from any minute now.

"Polo, Eddie loves you so much. You're like a brother to him."

"I know which is why I feel so horrible about the way I feel about you. That alone, and the fact that I love you, is why I drink so much. I just don't know how to deal with what I'm feeling."

"You don't love me Polo. Eddie loves me."

"And I do too. I probably love you even more than he does."

No.

Now that was impossible.

No one loved me as much as Eddie did.

"No you don't love me Polo."

"How are you going to tell me what I feel?"

"Well, if you do, you love me like a sister right?"

Polo looked at me.

"No. Because I couldn't do this to my sister," and before I could stop him, he kissed me.

And he kept kissing.

And finally...I kissed him back.

The way that he kissed me made my insides melt.

Had it not been for the Rum and coke on his lips and tongue, the kiss would have been perfect.

My body was telling me to take it to the next level but of course my mind reminded me that we couldn't.

Finally, after guilt started to set in and because I was becoming extremely aroused, I pulled away from him.

We both just sat there for a while and didn't say anything.

I didn't know what to say.

I didn't know what to do.

I'd just kissed my husband's best friend...

And I liked it too.

"Sassi, um, I'm sorry."

"You're sorry for what?"

My soul damn near left my body at the sound of Eddie's voice.

I'd felt Polo's body jump as well.

"I expected to find you hiding back here but not you Sassi. What are you sorry about Polo?" Eddie asked again.

"For giving her such an issue about hooking me up with this co-worker of hers. I was just telling her what we talked about earlier. About me really needing to find a wife and settling down. I guess I'm going to let her hook me up one last time and see what happens. Hopefully she will be the one."

Expert liar, I see.

"Oh bro, the one will come when its time. Don't rush it. Come on back in with me. The other fellas and I need your opinion," Eddie said and Polo immediately got up.

"You coming?" Eddie asked me, and I shook my head.

"No, I still need some fresh air. I'll be in soon."

Eddie nodded and he and Polo walked away.

Oh my goodness!

Did that really just happen?

I touched my lips, trying to forget the wrong that I'd done. But it felt so right.

It felt so good.

Get thee behind me Satan!

Ugh!

I just wanted to scream.

This was not supposed to be happening to me.

I was falling for my husband's best friend, and it was going to be harder than I thought to stop.

I sat there in a daze until I figured that something probably needed to be refilled or something, so I got up and headed towards the house.

How was I ever going to face Polo again?

Hell, how was I going to face my husband?

Entering the kitchen, I was met by Mama who was doing my job and refilling chip bowls and trays.

She didn't say anything, so I simply joined in.

But just as she was heading out of the kitchen, she spoke.

"I won't ask what you and Polo were doing behind that outhouse for those few minutes, but I will say this. The grass ain't always greener on the other side. Everybody always has something to hide," Mama said and she walked away.

Ugh…including me.

****

CHAPTER 4

"Can I take you to lunch?" Polo asked as I walked to my car.

I was actually happy to see him because we needed to talk.

"Eddie already knows. I told him that I was coming to see this "co-worker" of yours that you have supposedly been trying to set me up with and I told him that I was going to go ahead and treat you to lunch while I was here," Polo said.

Well, I guess now I had to go.

He opened his car door as I shut mine, and I got inside of Polo's car.

I was so nervous.

I felt like I was about to lose my virginity or something.

Hell, I wasn't even this nervous when that had happened.

We had been so awkward around each other since the kiss and I wasn't sure that being around him was such a good idea.

We drove in silence for a while and then an old school song came on the radio.

"Um, this song always reminds me of you. Think back, this was the song that you and Eddie listened to on your first date wasn't it?"

I thought hard.

Wait a minute…he was right.

When I got into Eddie's car, ten years ago for our first officially date, he was playing "Every time I close my eyes" by Babyface.

"Yeah, I know it was, because I told him to play it. I would close my eyes and see your face and then when Eddie told me the next day after the night at the bar that you gave him your number, this was the song that I was listening to. And ever since then, whenever I hear it, I think of you."

Polo, Polo, Polo!

"I'm telling you, you were supposed to be mine," Polo said, as he pulled up at the most expensive restaurant that he could find.

I didn't say anything.

I didn't know what to say.

"Um, sit on that side," I said to him as I took a seat.

"No, I want to sit beside you."

He waited for me to scoot over in the booth and he sat beside me.

The waiter asked what we wanted to drink and to my surprise Polo ordered water.

"You're not drinking?"

"No. I'm trying to stop."

I just looked at him.

"Why?"

"Because of you."

Because of me for what?

Surely he knew that my Daddy had been a drunk. I was sure that Eddie had given him the scoop a long time ago but on top of that, Polo and I had texted for about an hour about my Daddy, a few days ago, and why I felt the way that I did about him.

The conversation had gotten deep and actually Polo made me see a few things that I had never bothered to look at or consider before.

But there was no point in stopping for me.

He couldn't have me.

Eddie already did.

"So, about that kiss," he started.

"Polo, I don't want to talk about that. But I will say this. That can never happen again."

All I had been able to think about was that damn kiss and sometimes the thoughts of it made me smile.

But other times I frowned because I knew that it was wrong.

"Why not?"

"Really Polo?"

"Yes, really Sassi. I want you."

"You can't have me."

"Yes I can. I don't mind sharing you. If that's the only way that I can have you."

"You're talking crazy Polo," I rolled my eyes at him.

"Don't call me crazy. I hate when people call me crazy. I'm not crazy for wanting you."

"I'm married to your best friend."

"For now."

Was he serious?

The waiter came back with our drinks and asked for our orders.

I ordered a salad and I couldn't even recite what it was that Polo had ordered.

"No Polo, it was a mistake," I said as soon as the gentleman walked away.

"It didn't feel like a mistake to me. You kissed me back."

For some reason I wanted him to kiss me right then and there but I had to fight my flesh.

I was so confused by what I was feeling and I didn't like it one bit.

If I was going to cheat on my husband, why not find someone else to do it with?

Someone other than Polo.

Someone other than his best friend.

This was just wrong on so many levels.

I just couldn't do this to Eddie.

"We can't do this to Eddie Polo," I whined.

"I don't want to hurt him but I can't help how I feel."

He touched my thigh and I shivered.

"Don't touch me Polo."

"Stop me."

He slid his hand up my dress and towards my awaiting vagina and I squeezed my legs together.

"Open your legs."

"What?"

"I said open your legs."

I shook my head no.

"Open your legs Sassi," he whispered in my ear and my legs became disobedient and they opened on their own.

I started to shake.

I wanted to just get up and run out of there but my feet wouldn't let me.

They were frozen and they wouldn't cooperate to save my life.

Get up and get out of here stupid!

The voice in my head taunted me but I found a way to ignore it.

Polo found the side of my panties and his hand started to roam.

I swallowed, hard, as he touched the lips of my heated *puss*.

His fingers found the opening to my *watering hole*, and my juices drowned them instantly.

"Stop Polo," I whispered.

"Make me."

He was so close and I wanted to suck his lips off of his face.

His fingers moved swiftly.

In and out.

In and out.

Why did it have to feel so damn good?

I felt like I was about to pass out and I was struggling to breath.

"I wanna make love to you Sassi. Just once. And I promise we won't do it again. We won't hurt him again. Just one night with you is all I need."

I shook my head and it seemed to only make his fingers work harder.

He had lost his mind!

We definitely couldn't have sex.

There was no way that I was going to cross that line.

I squeezed my eyes closed and bit my bottom lip.

"Please stop."

"Just one time."

I was so turned on that I didn't know what to do with myself.

If I could take him into the bathroom and screw his brains out, I swear that I would.

See, if Eddie did random, spontaneous stuff like this, we would be okay.

This was exciting.

This is what I called keeping things spicy.

A little coochie fingering in a restaurant ain't ever hurt nobody!

I just hoped that Polo went to wash his hands before he touched his food.

In the very beginning, Eddie was somewhat spontaneous at times, but I guess he was only doing it because Polo had told him to.

I damn near had to pay Eddie to even kissed me in public.

Something like this was definitely out of the question.

"Just once."

"No."

"Just once. I need to feel you just once."

I shook my head again.

"I can't do it."

"One time."

I felt my body starting to heat up as I neared a sexual explosion, but I wouldn't allow it.

I just couldn't cum from Polo's hand.

I just couldn't do it.

"Stop Polo."

"Okay."

He stopped moving his fingers and waited to see what I would say or do next.

I struggled to catch my breath and then the sound of someone clearing their throat made me open my eyes.

Mama.

"Ma, um what are you doing here?"

I tried to move away from Polo, but he didn't move.

"I should be asking you two the same thing."

She stared at me.

"You guys are sitting a little close don't you think?"

At that moment, Polo moved his hand from between my legs and slid slightly to the right.

"Oh, we were just chatting."

"Hmmph, with your eyes closed? I stood there for about a minute and that looked like more than chatting."

"I was thinking."

"Well were you thinking or chatting?"

"Both."

"Sassi you have to come better than that. But I'll tell you one thing, I don't like this, whatever this is, and I don't approve of it."

"Approve of what Mrs. Sampson? There is nothing going on except conversation between friends."

"Stop trying to make me out to be stupid. I was born at night, but it damn sure wasn't last night," Mama snarled at both of us.

The waiter came back with our food and she waited until he walked away to finish her statement.

"And just so we're clear, I am telling Eddie about this."

Both Polo and I started talking at the same time, but Mama threw up her hand and walked away in disgust.

We both sat there, unsure of what to say next.

"She's not going to tell him for real is she?"

Honestly, I had no clue.

Usually when Mama said something, she meant it.

But I was hoping that this time was the exception.

But what was she telling anyway?

What that she saw us sitting close and that she thought we were a little too close for comfort?

That was pretty much all that she could say.

But knowing Mama, she would say much more.

"I gotta' get back to work."

Polo stood up and I stood up behind him.

He left a good bit of money on the table, right beside the untouched food and we left.

I called Mama over and over again but she wouldn't pick up her phone and Polo called Eddie to let him know that he was on his way to take me back to work.

I wasn't sure if Mama would actually tell Eddie or not.

I was hoping that she would at least talk to me first about what she thought she knew before running her mouth to my husband.

Arriving at work, Polo finally spoke to me directly.

"I love you Sassi."

I didn't say a word.

I simply got out of the car and headed in to work.

This was all a mistake.

One big, terrible mistake.

And I had a feeling that it was all about to blow up in my face.

And I was sure that Polo felt the same…

I smiled as my three men walked into the house and after kissing the boys, I waited for Eddie to kiss me, but he didn't.

"What's wrong with you?"

"You tell me," he said.

I looked at him.

Oh no!

Mama told him for real!

Why mama, why!

My stomach started bubbling and I wanted to throw up.

How dare she speak on something without having all of the facts?

I told the kids to go play as Eddie took a seat on the couch.

"Look Eddie, it's not what you think."

"It's exactly what I think."

Damn it Mama!

She had no business telling *my* husband anything.

It wasn't her place.

But it wasn't her fault it was mine.

"Look Eddie, It's not what you think. I'm so---,"

"Oh yes it is. Polo got to take the most beautiful woman in the world to lunch today. But lucky me, I get to take her to dinner," Eddie smiled.

What?

I let out a deep breath as he hugged me.

"What? What is it Sassi?"

I continued to breathe.

He had me fooled.

I was about to tell on myself and he wasn't even talking about the situation.

"Nothing baby."

"Oh, your Mama called me a few times today. Did she call you? I missed her calls and when I called her back, she didn't answer."

Thank goodness.

And Mama really was going to tell him, I couldn't say that I was surprised.

"Yeah. She was looking for me and because I was busy at work today and not answering her phone calls, she must have called you to see if you could get in touch with me."

"Oh."

"Now since I don't have to cook tonight, let's get this whole dinner on you thing on the ball shall we?"

Eddie smiled and headed to get the boys.

I sat down for a second to steady my heartbeat.

What if I'd told on myself?

What if Mama had succeeded in telling Eddie what she assumes that she saw today between Polo and I?

This whole doing whatever with another man, just wasn't for me; especially when it's with someone as close to my husband as Polo.

This was clearly a sign that things were out of hand already and I needed to get myself together.

I needed to put Polo in his place before we got ourselves into something that we couldn't get out of.

I thought about the outhouse incident and what went on at the restaurant.

Nothing like that could ever happen again.

Even if I secretly wanted it to.

And now that we'd crossed yet another line, it was going to be harder than ever for us to get back to where we used to be as just friends.

Damn.

That was the only way to keep us both from hurting Eddie was that Polo had to go.

That was the only way that I was going to be able to keep my legs closed.

I'd always wondered about Polo and if his sex was as good as the women acted that I'd known him to deal with and here lately, I'd found myself wanting to find out first hand.

But I knew that I couldn't.

And I had to make sure that I wouldn't.

Polo had to go.

Someway, somehow, Polo just had to go.

But how?

And what about Mama?

I had to get to her before she got to Eddie.

Picking up Eddie's phone, I spammed her number to block her from calling him.

That would hold off for a little while.

But if she popped up, now that would be a different story.

"You ready?"

I grinned at my husband.

"Yep."

~***~

"If you don't tell him, I will."

"Tell him what? There's nothing to tell."

Mama had stayed away for about a week or so but I knew that it was only a matter of time before she popped up to give her two cents.

"Are you and Polo having an affair?"

"No. I swear on my life and on the kids life Polo and I have never had sex Mama."

She looked at me.

"Then what is it then? And I want the truth this time."

I exhaled.

I didn't want to tell her the truth but if I didn't, she was going to tell my husband what she thought that she knew.

I could see it in her eyes.

"It's nothing Ma. Polo and I have been around each other for years. I was feeling a little disconnected from my marriage and---,"

"You started to see something in him that isn't really there. Sassi, marriage isn't easy. You saw what I went through with your father. But you have a good husband. You have a great family. Go to counseling, work it out. Don't ruin it by looking for what you're not getting at home in another man; especially not in your husband's best friend."

I knew Mama was right and I was trying to work things out.

Polo and I hadn't talked in over a week and he hadn't even came by the house.

Eddie invited him for dinner just the other night, but Polo declined.

He'd said that he had plans already but I was sure that he was avoiding me just like I had been avoiding him.

He had to feel just as guilty as I did.

"Ma, I have everything under control. I'm not going to ruin my marriage. My boys need their father and no matter what, I love my husband."

"Then start acting like it," Mama said and she pulled out of the drive way.

She'd pulled up right behind me after work, so I didn't have a chance to avoid her.

I still had over an hour or so to myself before Eddie and the kids came home so I headed into the house so that I could try to get an hour worth of writing done before I had to turn into somebody's wife and somebody's mama for the rest of the evening.

Just as I sat down at the desk, I heard the front door open behind me.

"I thought she was never going to leave."

Polo said as he sat in the chair closest to me.

I felt frightened for some reason at the sight of him. I didn't trust him and I didn't trust myself around him.

"So, I tried to stay away but I can't. Did you think about what I said?"

I looked at him confused.

"We should make love one time. We both want it. We can get it out of our systems and never do it again."

"No Polo."

He stood up and I jumped to my feet.

He came closer to me and I moved but he didn't care.

"Kiss me."

"No."

He walked closer.

"It's hot in here," I cleared my throat and tried to walk past him but he stopped me.

I tried to pull away from him but he tightened his grip.

He wrapped his arms around my waist and allowed me to try to wiggle free of him, but he knew that I wasn't going anywhere.

He started kissing on my neck and licking on my ears.

After a while, I stopped fighting and just stood there.

My knees started to buckle and Polo turned his attention to my face and placed his nose up against mine.

I tried to catch my breath.

I tried to convince my body not to want him.

But my body and my heart never could agree these days and soon I gave in and indulged in Polo's passionate kisses.

We kissed until there was nothing left to do except take it to the next level.

Polo lifted my skirt and ripped my panties at the sides.

He kissed me and in one swift motion he picked me up off of my feet and wrapped my legs around him, just before sitting down on the couch.

We kissed and I grinded up against him.

I could feel his *pipe* swelling underneath me and finally he headed to unzip his pants and he freed himself.

He lifted my shirt and pulled out my left breast and placed it into his mouth.

He sucked the nipple of it forcefully as I closed my eyes and concentrated on the feeling.

My juices escaped from my vagina by the galloons and I couldn't remember the last time that I'd wanted a piece of *wood* so badly.

I felt Polo touch himself and he led the head of his penis to my throbbing *opening.*

But just as I was about to sit on it, my phone ranged on the arm of the chair and unintentionally glancing at it, Eddie's face popped up.

Eddie.

Oh no.

I jumped off of Polo and reached for the phone.

"Hello."

"Hey baby. I'm on my way home. Why are you out of breath?"

I breathed heavily as I placed my breast back into my bra and pulled down my skirt.

"I was in the kitchen and I ran to the phone."

"Oh. Well, I'm stopping to get the kids now and I'll be there shortly."

I hung up and looked back at Polo to see that he had gotten himself together too.

"Get out Polo. And don't come back here. I don't know what you are going to tell Eddie, but don't you come back here. Or I'll tell him the truth. I'll tell him what's been going on between the two of us. I'll make him choose. Whether he believes me or believes you it doesn't matter. But I swear I will tell him. Just go away."

We had to stop this.

I walked off as Polo let himself out.

I washed off in a hurry and put on some panties.

I headed back to the living room to find the ones that Polo had ripped off but I couldn't find them.

He must have taken them with him.

Pervert.

I grabbed some perfume and sprayed it all over my body and all over the living room to get rid of Polo's scent.

And then I headed to the kitchen to start dinner like nothing had happened.

For some reason, I started to cry.

I wasn't sure why.

I wasn't sure if it was because I had come so close to having sex with Polo or because I couldn't believe that I would actually let things get so far out of hand.

"Hey honey!" I heard Eddie yell and I hurriedly dried my eyes.

I placed on a smile and turned around.

"Hey."

I kissed Eddie and then I kissed the boys.

They headed to the refrigerator, got juice and a snack and ran off to watch TV.

"Did Polo come by here? I passed him not far from here. I blew the horn but he didn't see me."

"Nope. He didn't come by."

"Oh. Well. I missed you today. I couldn't wait to get home to you," he said and kissed me again.

"Oh really? Well, what are you going do about it?"

Eddie grinned and kissed me again.

I placed down the knife that I was holding and wrapped my arms around him.

Eddie was a better kisser than Polo.

Not that I should have been comparing them, but he was.

"I wish you could take me right here, right now," I said to him.

"And why can't I?"

I looked at him.

Was he trying to be freaky?

Was he trying to be spontaneous?

He turned me around to face the opening of the kitchen and placed my hands on the huge island in the middle of the floor.

"What about the kids?"

"You know what time it is. That show stays on for thirty minutes. They watch it every day and they never move until it goes off. Besides, we can hear them and we can see them if they come. Just don't scream too loud," Eddie said, rubbing his hard penis up against my butt.

"You don't need a pill?"

"Nope. I don't need it," he said and lifted up my skirt.

Oh my, hopefully he didn't.

Since Polo already had me in the mood, I would probably cum in just minutes, even if that was all that Eddie had to offer.

I arched my back and bent over as he started to tug on my panties but he stopped.

"Why did you change your panties?"

"What?"

"Your panties were leopard this morning. Now they are pink. Why did you change them?"

"No, they were pink."

Eddie cleared his throat and I turned to face him.

"They were leopard Sassi. I watched you put them on. Why did you change them?"

"You're mistaken Eddie. They were pink. I didn't change them."

He looked at me and I looked down at the floor.

"They were leopard Sassi. But whatever you say," he said and he walked away.

It wasn't until about two minutes later that I actually moved.

What could have been a beautiful moment for us was ruined in only a matter of seconds.

I should have said that I washed up after work.

But he would have wanted to know why.

If I had changed my clothes I could have said that I washed up and changed because I was sweaty or something.

It happened so fast and it hadn't crossed my mind that Eddie had been paying attention when I'd gotten dressed that morning.

This was confirmation that Eddie wasn't dumb, not even a little bit, and if I even thought that I was going to be able to cheat and he not notice, I was in for a rude awakening.

Eddie didn't say much during dinner or for the rest of the night.

When I'd gotten out of the shower, I'd caught him going through my underwear drawer.

He must have been looking for the leopard panties, but they weren't there.

Some that were similar were, so maybe he thought that they were the pair that I'd had on.

Once we were in bed he finally spoke.

"Are you having an affair Sassi?"

"What? No."

"It's because of the sex isn't? Because I wasn't satisfying you or because I had to start taking the pills?" Eddie said.

"No Eddie. I am not having an affair. I wouldn't do that to you. I love you."

Eddie didn't respond for a long while.

And then his next words took my breath away.

And not in a good way.

"I love you too, but that doesn't mean a thing. If you are thinking about it, cheating on me, you had better hope that it's worth it. I will leave you Sassi. And I will take the boys with me."

And he meant it.

~***~

Of course I wouldn't let Eddie take my boys without a fight, but who would want to put their kids through something like that?

I sure as hell didn't.

A nasty court battle or divorce weren't exactly in my plans and being that Eddie was an accountant, there was no telling who he knew.

He could be handling the monies of lawyers and even judges, and there was no telling what type of leverage he might have or what strings they might be able to pull for a friend.

And despite almost having sex with Polo, I still loved Eddie more than anything in the world.

"Girl, he is still acting strange."

"Because he's not stupid. What are you going to do?"

"I can't mess up my marriage or put my kids through a divorce. And I'll be damned if Eddie thinks that he would be able to take them and keep them from me."

Micki frowned.

"Did you tell Patrice?"

"Nope. I don't want to hear her mouth. Please don't tell her."

Telling Micki to keep her mouth shut was like telling her not to breathe, but maybe I would get lucky.

Patrice's judgmental ass would have more than enough to say and irrelevant opinions that I really wasn't in the mood to hear.

Not to mention the fact that she'd told me before I married Eddie that he wasn't the one.

She could see it too but I didn't listen to her.

I listened to Mama instead.

"Well, Polo needs to be on the same page. He needs to understand how serious this could become. Both of you guys love Eddie; hell, even your kids are his god-kids and I know that he wouldn't want to see them go through something like that. Maybe you should tell him what Eddie said and then put this behind you. Hopefully things will go back to normal."

"Even normal wasn't all that great," I said to her.

"Yeah, but at least you weren't at risk of losing your family."

She was right.

Micki was a single mother and my brother didn't do the best job with helping her like he was supposed to nor did her other kid's father.

I didn't want to end up like her.

I wanted my family.

I needed my husband.

And so I needed to talk to Polo.

Micki and I finished our lunch, and I called work to tell them that I had an emergency and that I needed to leave for the rest of the day.

Forwarding all of my work phone calls to my cell phone, just in case Eddie called, I headed to see Polo.

Polo lived in a huge house, in an upscale neighborhood.

I hadn't been inside of his house in so long that I almost didn't remember what it looked like.

I had been by, but hadn't been inside in quite some time.

I got out of the car and walked slowly to the door.

The garage door was closed so I wasn't sure if his cars were in there so I ranged the doorbell.

I reached for my phone to call him, but just as I did, he opened the door.

He looked at me and I tried not to notice that he was only wearing a wife beater and briefs.

"Uh, can we talk?"

He moved to the side so that I could come in.

"Could you put some clothes on please," I said to him, heading to the overpriced couch in the living room.

It was nice and super clean.

You would have thought that he had a maid or something, but he didn't.

I looked around as he sat in the recliner, ignoring my request.

I noticed my torn panties on the coffee table.

I stuffed them in my purse.

Nasty.

"Look, Eddie noticed that I switched my panties. He questioned me."

Polo looked concerned.

"I told him that he was wrong and that he was mistaken. And he told me that if he caught me having an affair, he was going to leave me and take the kids with him."

Polo's face softened.

"Okay."

"Okay what?"

"Okay, I'll leave you alone. I've been living with my feelings for you for years and not acting on them. I know how to do it. I just didn't want to."

I looked at him.

Well, that was easier than I thought.

"But I'll do it under one condition."

Uh oh.

Here we go.

"Let me feel you. Right here. Right now. And we will pretend like it never happened and Eddie will never find out. And you'll never have to worry about me coming on to you again. I swear."

I looked at him.

He stood up and pulled down his briefs.

For the first time, I was actually staring at his manhood and it was actually bigger than it had felt when I was grinding on it.

It was standing at attention and he started to stroke it.

I sat there, in somewhat of a daze.

And then I covered my eyes.

After a second, I slid my fingers apart, just a little, so that I could get another look at it.

Leave Sassi. Just get up and leave.

But I couldn't move.

I didn't get up and I wasn't even sure that I wanted to.

Maybe just once would take away the curiosity.

Just once and then we could never do this to Eddie again.

Polo walked over to me.

"Stand up and take your panties off."

I still just sat there.

Should I do this?

Of course not.

But I wanted to.

Damn it.

I really wanted to do this.

Polo moved my hands away from my eyes, and his pipe was only barely an inch away from my face.

To get the penis out of my face, I stood up, slowly.

"I want you."

I just couldn't do it.

"Touch it."

My hand touched his rod and immediately I knew that there was no turning back.

"Eddie can never find out about this Polo," I said.

He didn't comment.

He unzipped the back of my skirt and slid it down my legs, along with my underwear.

I just stood there.

We both did.

"I love you Sassi."

"Stop saying that."

He didn't love me, at least not in that way.

This had nothing to do with love.

He pushed me back down on the couch and then got on his knees.

He slid me closer to him, putting my legs on his shoulders.

"Polo, wait, maybe…"

And that was it.

He put his mouth on me and I must say that I was impressed.

He moved his tongue faster and faster until he heard me scream.

I didn't even try to hide the fact that I was enjoying it.

For just a second I forgot that he wasn't my husband and I enjoyed the pleasures of another man's mouth for the first time in years.

He moved abruptly and pulled me to the floor.

He just stared between my legs for a second and then he stood up.

"Don't move."

I laid there, not moving, and Polo returned with a condom tightly hugging his *pole*.

Without even hesitating, or giving me a chance to change my mind, he damn near dived in between my legs and entered me.

"Ohhh," I squealed.

I looked at Polo.

He looked deep into my eyes as he went deeper and deeper.

I cooed as he took my legs and placed them on his shoulders.

"Um," he said as he started to stroke.

He pumped inside of me slowly as though he wanted to take his time.

I moved my hips and I squealed as things started to get wild.

It felt so good.

It felt damn good.

I felt as though I was trying to rush myself to the finish line, but my insides wanted to savor the moment.

They seemed to want to enjoy every second of this "one time" thing.

And what a "one time" thing that it was.

Polo put me in so many different positions that I felt like I was some kind of porn star.

It was as though he wanted to experience sex with me in every way that he could and I let him have his way with me.

"Get on your knees."

He got behind me and he pumped so hard and so fast that I struggled to keep my balance.

After a while, and realizing that I didn't have a good excuse to explain carpet burn to my husband, I gave up and fell to my stomach.

But Polo stayed behind me, and stayed in my stomach too, giving me some of the best dick that I had ever had.

"Are you going to cum for me?" Polo asked.

I bit my bottom lip.

"Are you going to nut for *daddy*?" Polo said.

"Yes. Yes. Yes!"

And just as the last yes came out of my mouth, I *came* aggressively, and so did Polo.

Before I had a chance to catch my breath, Polo spoke.

"You have to go."

Polo's words caught me by surprise.

But I didn't say anything.

I got up, got myself together and I headed out the door.

It wasn't until I was in my car that reality hit and I realized that I'd just betrayed my husband in the worst way.

I'd just had sex with his "brother", his friend.

What the hell was I thinking!

Knock. Knock.

What….

I thought I'd seen a ghost and my heart felt as though it was about to beat out of my chest.

Eddie.

I rolled down my car window.

"What are you doing here?"

Think.

Think.

Think.

"I just got here. I was coming to talk to Polo."

Eddie looked at me.

"For what?"

"Um, I came to talk to him about you."

Eddie looked angry.

I would rather him be angry about that than about what Polo and I had just done.

"I came to get some advice or to ask him to talk to you. We have been in a weird place lately because of the panty issue and I wanted Polo's advice on how to get through to you and make you believe me."

"You don't have the right to discuss any of our personal matters with my friends Sassi."

Just then Polo walked outside.

He was fully dressed.

He walked over to the car.

"Hey man. Sassi what are you doing here?" He asked me as though everything was fine.

Eddie answered for me and filled him in.

"Go back to work Sassi. Come on man let's go eat," Eddie said to Polo and they headed to my husband's car.

They pulled off and I just sat there, trying to recover from what felt like a mini heart attack.

Polo must have known that Eddie was on his way; which is why he'd told me to get out of his house.

What if he had come while I was still inside?

I tried not to think about it as I drove away.

I figured that Polo had timed everything in his head, just right, before even making his first move.

I didn't go back to work as Eddie had instructed.

Instead, I hurried home, washed my panties out in the sink, threw them in the dryer and washed up.

I was sure that Eddie had paid attention to them that day too, so I had to make sure that I covered all of the bases.

As I stood in front of the dryer, I reminisced on Polo's touch and on the way that he had felt inside of me.

I knew now why women were crazy about him.

I had to give it to him…his sex was good!

Though the sex hadn't been on the stalker, crazy type of level, it was good enough to make you crave for more.

I scowled myself as I checked to see if my panties were dry.

I'd just cheated on my husband.

And I'd enjoyed every minute of it.

Oh my…

I was going straight to hell!

Putting on my dry panties, I headed to the living room.

Damn it Eddie!

This was his fault.

All of the issues with him had led up to this very moment.

But the moment was over and now it was time to work on my forever.

Now I could focus back on my marriage.

I could try to make it better.

But Eddie was going to have to help me because what happened with Polo would not happen again.

And I was going to make sure of it.

****

CHAPTER 5

"It didn't work."

I looked at Polo.

"Sex only made me want you more. I'm going crazy. Every time Eddie touches you, I feel like I want to kill him."

I looked at him as though he was speaking a foreign language.

"Get out of my face Polo," I said to him and walked towards the door.

Eddie and the boys were washing the car and I was bringing them lunch.

Polo offered to help me carry out the sandwiches.

"Sassi, I want you. Tell me you don't want me again."

"I don't want you."

"I don't believe you."

"Well, you should."

I walked outside as Polo continued to talk but he stopped abruptly as Eddie smiled at us.

I sat the drinks on the hood of Polo's car and he sat the sandwiches beside it.

Eddie waited until I was far enough from the food and out of nowhere he slung water off of the rag in my direction.

Was he trying to be fun?

"Really Eddie?"

He picked up the water hose.

"Really what?"

Eddie pointed the hose at me.

"I wish you would. You wouldn't dare," I said to him.

"Hmm, let's see about that!"

Eddie sprayed me and I mean he sprayed me good.

I ran towards him, drenched in water, yet he kept on spraying.

He started to laugh once I reached him and tried to swing on him.

The boys laughed and joined in on the fun as Eddie and I wrestled over the hose.

Finally Eddie gave up and I sprayed him and the kids as the hollered in laughter and attempt to run for cover.

Soak and wet, I stopped and Eddie came closer to me.

He was smiling and so was I.

"Oh, I love you Sassi."

"I love you too baby."

We kissed and the kids acted as though they had just saw us naked or something.

"We're going to be okay."

"I hope so."

Things weren't exactly normal between us yet, but his comment had just given me a ton of hope.

We were going to make it through this.

Every marriage goes through something, it was just our turn.

Heading to reach them all a drink, I almost forgot that Polo was there.

He was now sitting on the porch, staring at us.

I could see how uncomfortable he was and he may have even been a little hurt by watching us share a moment.

Scratch that, there was fire in his eyes, but he had to get over it.

I walked towards him with a glass and a sandwich.

"Here you go," he said.

"This is supposed to be my family. Not his. You are supposed to be mine," he whispered.

"You're welcome," I said loud enough for Eddie to hear and headed back in his direction.

He'd agreed to one time and he wasn't getting anything else from me.

Not now.

And not ever.

~***~

"What?"

"Nothing."

"What bitch?"

"Nothing."

Micki looked at me for a second and then she gasp.

"You did it didn't you?"

"Did what?"

"Polo."

"No. Why would you say that?"

Though I told her everything, this was one of those things that I was keeping to myself.

At least I tried to.

"Tell me."

"There's nothing to tell."

"If you don't tell me, I will ask him," she smirked.

"Yeah right."

She folded her arms.

"Okay. We did."

"Did what?"

"Had sex."

She placed her hands over her mouth.

"No you didn't!"

I nodded and proceeded with filling her in with the details.

She listened attentively and even made a few noises here and there.

"So now what?"

"Now nothing. We will never do it again. It's out of my system. I love Eddie and I don't want to mess up my marriage. It was one time. Polo will never touch me again."

"Never say never."

"Never."

And I was serious too.

I left Micki's house in a hurry.

I ignored Polo's call for the tenth time that day.

I didn't want to talk to him.

What else was there to talk about?

I had cut out all of the constant text messaging, the sneaking on the phone with him and everything.

We had an agreement and I was sticking to it.

He hung up and started calling me Private as though I didn't already know that it was him.

I ignored the first few calls but he just wouldn't stop.

The next time the private call came across the screen, I answered it.

"What is it Polo? I told you that it was only one time! Now please stop calling me!"

"This isn't Polo."

Oops!

"Hey mama."

"What was one time Sassi?"

"Nothing. Why are you calling me private mama?"

"You don't answer my calls when I call you Sassi. Your brother told me about private calling."

I was going to stab him!

"What was one time?"

I pitched her some story about me covering for Polo and pretending to be his girl-friend to run off one of his stalking sex buddies.

I had become one heck of a good liar and from the looks of it my explanation was enough to get mama off of my back.

She said a few words, but overall it wasn't much.

As I entered the grocery store, I hung up with her, dropped my phone in my purse and then put it on my shoulder.

Just as I grabbed a buggy and started to push it, some woman walked up from behind me and bumped me.

She bumped me so hard that I had to check to make sure that my arm was still connected to my body.

Oww!

She continued walking, and I screamed after her.

"Damn! Excuse you!"

But she never turned around.

She never said a word, she just kept walking.

After rubbing my shoulder for a while, I headed to pick up a few things for dinner.

I looked for the woman down each aisle so I could give her a piece of my mind, but I never saw her.

It was like she had just vanished.

After paying for my things, walking out of the grocery store, I noticed a police officer with a dog standing right near the exit.

At the sight of me, the dog started to bark.

He acted as though he wanted to eat me for dinner and I hurriedly tried to get away from him, but the policeman started to follow me.

"Excuse me ma'am, can I talk to you for a minute?"

I looked at the officer once I'd reached my car.

"Yes?"

The dog continued to bark and I wondered why the officer wasn't trying to calm him down.

"Do you have any drugs on you ma'am?"

I looked at him like he was stupid.

"What? No. I don't do drugs officer."

"My K-9 is trained and a part of the drug task force. He only acts this way when drugs are involved."

"Like I said, I don't do drugs. I don't have drugs. Maybe your dog is on drugs. I know my rights, and so with that I will say, good day officer," I said and got into the car.

I thought that things were going to get out of hand and I surely thought that he was going to try to search me or be nasty about the situation because of my smart comment, but he didn't do a thing.

He let me drive off with no problem.

Once I was home, I sat there to think about the officer and his dog.

I wouldn't dare have any drugs.

I didn't even drink unless my husband wanted me to have a drink with him; which was very rare.

My phone started to ring and I opened my huge purse to find it.

I moved things around and finally I found it.

But that wasn't the only thing that I found.

I lifted up the Ziploc bag and stared at it.

I opened it to sniff it.

Yep.

It was weed alright.

And a good bit of it.

What the hell?

How the hell?

Huh?

How did that get in there?

I'd just switched purses that morning so I was sure that it hadn't been in there before.

So how did it get there?

At Micki's I'd left my purse in the car.

The only place that'd I'd carried it was at the grocery store.

The grocery store.

Hmmm…

The woman that almost bumped me to the hospital did come from behind me.

Could she have dropped it into my purse during the process?

It seemed a little farfetched but how else would it have gotten there?

Maybe she'd noticed the officer and dog once she'd come in and tried to get rid of it.

I wasn't sure but I was so glad that the officer hadn't searched me.

I would have surely gone to jail.

I got out of the car with my groceries and threw the bag of weed in the big trashcan.

Polo called my phone just as I entered the house, but I sent him to the voicemail again.

After wat could have just happened to me, the Man above must still be on my side; so any sinning with Polo was definitely out of the question.

I needed all of the mercy that I could possibly get.

~***~

"You're the girl from the video," she said.

"Excuse me?"

She smiled and walked closer.

"You used to fool around with Polo right? He and I get down every once and a while, and he'd wanted to watch some of his homemade videos to get him in the mood. You were on the one that we watched yesterday," she said.

What!

I know damn well that Polo hadn't video tapped us having sex!

"I'm sorry, but you have me confused with someone else," I said to her.

"Are you sure? You look a lot like her. Do you even know Polo?"

"No. I'm afraid I don't."

"Oh, well, my bad," she said and walked away.

As soon as I was finished with my lunch, I dialed Polo's number as I walked out of the café.

"Why have you been ignoring me Sassi? I miss you."

"Miss me my ass! Did you video tape us having sex Polo?"

I was furious and I waited on him to respond before driving off.

"No. Who told you that?"

"Apparently some chick that you were screwing yesterday. She ran into me and said that she watched me on one of your sex tapes. How? I didn't see any camera. We hadn't even planned on getting down that day. I swear if you---,"

"I didn't tape you Sassi."

"You better hope that you didn't Polo, bye!"

"No, Sassi, wait."

"What? What is it?"

"You don't have to act like you hate me just because we fooled around do you?"

"I don't hate you Polo. That's the problem. I don't hate you at all. I just wish that things could go back to the way that they used to be."

"Your wish is my command."

Polo hung up and I got out of the car to go back into work. Hopefully he would stick to his word…

Once I was home that day, for some reason all I wanted to do was write.

It was as though I had to let all of my frustration out and what better place to do it than in my book.

I wrote as much as I could until I heard the front door open.

I stopped writing and turned around to greet my family.

The boys first, and then Eddie.

"How was your day?"

"Better now," I said to him as he kissed my forehead.

"You were writing?"

"Yeah, but I'm done. I'll get dinner started."

"No."

Eddie held his finger up at me, scrolled up the document a few hundred words and started to read.

He read for a few minutes and then he grinned at me.

"Keep writing. I'll go get pizza."

Aww!

He was finally being supportive.

It meant so much to me to have him behind me on something that I wanted to do so badly.

"Thank you Eddie. Thank you."

We just might have a shot at this.

He was really putting forth an effort and I really did appreciate it.

I wrote until it was time to eat and even after everyone had eaten, Eddie offered to bathe the boys and get them ready for bed.

He encouraged me to write for another hour or so and said that if he fell asleep before I came to bed, to wake him and say good night.

But I had other plans for him.

We hadn't had sex in a long time.

Since Eddie was positive that I had changed my panties and that I was having an affair, or at least thinking about it, he hadn't even tried to touch me.

There were occasions that it seemed as though we both wanted it, but neither of us made the first move.

But tonight I was going to.

I wrote for a while and went to find Eddie.

He was in the shower, so I went to kiss the boys and then headed to shower in their bathroom.

After a few minutes, I stepped out of the shower and headed to our bedroom, soak and wet.

Eddie stared at me once I entered.

I walked over to him.

He looked at me with so much love in his eyes that I knew that all along, he was all that I needed.

No one was ever going to love me the way that he did.

No one was ever going to value me, and respect me like Eddie did.

"I love you."

"I love you too."

"I didn't take a pill Sassi."

"It's okay baby. You don't need one."

"What if it happens again?"

"It won't."

I kissed him.

Even if it did, I wouldn't care.

Tonight was about him.

Tonight was about making him feel good.

Tonight was about me showing him that I was sorry; even if he didn't know exactly what I was sorry for.

And although Eddie ended up lasting for only about five minutes, I had never been more satisfied in all of my life.

Sex was important in a relationship, but it was all about compromise.

With him snoring beside me, I turned on the TV to watch the news.

I sat up at the face on the screen.

No. It couldn't be.

It was the woman from earlier that day; the woman that told me that she'd watched me on camera having sex with Polo.

She was dead.

She had been involved in a fatal hit and run.

There were no witnesses and she had been pronounced dead at the scene.

Coincidence?

Hmm…

The more and more I thought about it, I was sure that it was.

Even Polo wasn't that crazy.

I turned the TV off and snuggled under Eddie.

As he pulled me closer to him, in his arms I'd never felt so complete.

And I was going to love my wrong, yet so right, husband forever.

~***~

"So, what have I missed?" Patrice asked.

She was home for a little while and I hadn't realized how valuable her presence was until she was gone.

"Nothing much."

"Everything good at home?"

"Oh yes!"

And I wasn't lying either.

Everything was great.

Things were better than ever between Eddie and I.

Polo and I weren't screwing around or even talking behind Eddie's back anymore, so as far as I was concerned, things couldn't be better.

Polo was coming around as usual but he hadn't been inappropriate with me or even flirted with me in a long while.

I guess he finally got the hint.

Eddie and I were fine.

He was still taking the pills once or twice a week.

That was enough for me.

I wouldn't be greedy.

I was just trying to stay married.

"You know, I've been thinking that maybe I do need to find a man or something."

I knew that eventually she would.

Hell, no one wanted to be alone forever.

"Well, whoever the lucky man is, he will be getting a hand full. But he will be one lucky bastard," I said and Patrice beamed.

"Well, I have to head home. I have plans tonight," she said.

We blew kisses through the air and she was gone.

I also had to get started cleaning and cooking.

Polo was coming for dinner so of course I had to prepare to cook extra, not to mention that the house was a mess.

A few hours later, the house was clean, dinner was done, and Eddie answered the door.

Polo walked in, but he didn't walk in alone.

He walked in with Patrice.

Eddie and I both somewhat stared at them.

Eddie wasn't as fond of Patrice as he was of Micki.

They had never had any issues or anything, but he too thought that Patrice was a pain in the ass most of the time.

Polo and I made eye contact for only a second, but we both looked away as Eddie spoke.

"So, you guys are…"

"Friends."

"Yeah, just friends. For now," Patrice added.

I hadn't told her about Polo and I having sex.

And now I probably never would.

I had told her about Polo's flirting, but that was it.

"You could have told me all of this earlier," I said to her.

"Well, you know me. I like the element of surprise."

And the night was about to get interesting.

The room seemed incredibly tight for some reason and I barely said a word as everyone else chatted over dinner.

Polo was being disgustingly attentive to Patrice.

He was flirting with her.

Finishing her sentences.

Feeding her and even whispering things in her ear that made her giggle.

And you damn right I felt some kind of way!

I know, I know, I probably shouldn't have.

And I didn't have a clue as to why it was bothering me, but it did.

Eddie and I sat damn near miles apart as we watched them be all close and intimate.

I couldn't wait for the night to come to an end and when it finally did, I didn't even see Polo or Patrice to the door.

I lied and said that I wasn't feeling well and Eddie let them out.

A little while later he joined me in our bedroom.

"You okay?"

I nodded.

But something told me that he kind of knew that I wasn't.

"Polo and Patrice? Eww," Eddie said as he headed to the bathroom.

That's right.

Eww!

Polo knew just what he was doing and I was going to make sure that he didn't get away with it.

~***~

I exhaled.

Polo made himself comfortable beside me.

Every single time that we had sex, I felt like I wanted to die.

I hadn't kept my word.

That night that he'd shown up with Patrice had me in my feelings and I called him the next day to give him a piece of my mind.

Somehow I ended up at his house, and the rest was history.

What was supposed to have happened between us only once had now happened so many times that I'd lost count.

Of course he'd admitted that he wasn't really interested in Patrice and that he'd just wanted to piss me off.

It worked.

He'd told Patrice that there was simply nothing there that same day after we'd had sex, as I laid right beside of him.

She didn't say anything and didn't really even seem bothered by his words.

All she said was okay.

But I should have just left well enough alone because now I was definitely in too deep.

We had been having sex now, regularly for the past two months, and I was hooked like a fish.

It was becoming harder and harder to hide it from Eddie and if I douched with vinegar and water, one more time to tighten back up my coochie, I was sure that I was going to start pissing it.

We had gone too far.

We were doing too much and now there was an even bigger problem.

I was definitely falling in love with Polo, and I knew that I was in trouble.

I couldn't believe it and I wasn't proud of it, but I was falling for Polo every single time that he touched me.

Every time that he held me or told me a joke.

Every time that he gave me a book idea or gave me his opinions on my work.

I was falling hard for him but no matter what, I never stopped loving my husband.

Now, I just loved his best friend too.

My nerves were shot to shingles and I was so stressed out that I felt like I was going to croak over and die any minute now.

"I love you," Polo said.

I never said it back though I felt it.

I got up out of Polo's bed, washed up so that I could head back to work.

I was supposed to be on lunch; yet Polo had been the only one doing any eating.

"Give me a kiss," he said.

I kissed him.

"We gotta stop this," I mumbled.

"Oh lord, here we go with this again," Polo groaned.

"What do you mean? We can't keep doing this to him Polo," I said to him pitifully.

"Hell, it ain't like he ain't ever did it to you," Polo said.

Immediately his face expression told me that he'd just put his foot in his mouth.

What?

What the hell did he mean?

"What does that mean Polo?"

"Nothing."

"Are you telling me that Eddie has cheated on me?"

"No."

"Then what did you mean?"

"Nothing."

I let out a deep breath.

He was lying.

Polo knew something and he was trying to hide it.

But that just couldn't be true.

Eddie wouldn't do that to me.

"When Polo? When? And who?"

"That came out wrong. He hasn't cheated on you Sassi," he recanted but I knew that he was covering for him.

"Liar!"

I grabbed my purse and my keys and headed out of his bedroom for the door.

Naked, Polo chased after me.

He reached for my arm as I reached for the door, but to my surprise, someone else had beaten me to it.

Eddie.

Eddie looked at me and then at Polo.

Polo was still naked, considering that he hadn't bothered to put any clothes on.

Oh no!

Oh no, no, no, no!

This could not be happening right now.

"I just had to see it for myself. You've been coming here, twice a week, for a while now. I just had to see it for myself."

Polo and I both started talking at the same time, and I started to cry.

But at the sight of Eddie pulling out the gun, I started to scream.

"Eddie. Look. Wait."

But he wasn't listening to me.

He aimed it at Polo's face and then he lowered it towards his penis and fired.

He'd actually pulled the trigger.

Polo attempted to dodge the bullet it but it struck him in the thigh.

Eddie aimed the gun at him again but I jumped in front of Polo this time.

"No Eddie, please. You're not a killer. No. Don't do this. I'm so sorry baby. I'm so sorry."

Eddie looked at me as though he wanted shoot me too.

Or beat the crap out of me with the gun instead.

But he didn't.

Instead, he spit in my face and yelled to the top of his lungs.

"Go to hell Sassi!"

"Bro! Eddie!" Polo screamed out in pain, bleeding and everything but Eddie walked away.

As he passed by my car, he started to kick it.

Over and over again.

He punched out my driver's side window with his bare hands and it seemed as though he was doing everything to it that he wanted to do to me.

He fired the gun at two of my tires, causing them to go flat immediately and then he turned around and fired the gun twice at Polo's house.

One bullet hit right near my head as I stood in the doorway and the other one flew through the living room window.

"Eddie!" Polo continued to scream, but Eddie couldn't hear him.

I cried and called out to my husband too but he didn't answer either of us.

I walked towards him.

"Come any closer to me and I'll blow your damn brains out," Eddie snarled.

I'd never heard him sound so cold before, I'd never seen him so angry.

But I knew not to take his threat lightly.

Always listen to the man holding the gun.

Hell, I didn't even know that he had a gun.

Sirens wailed in the distance and I was sure that Polo had made his way to the phone to call the ambulance for help.

"Eddie please. It's not what you think."

"I think my wife and my best friend have been having an affair and you tell me that it's not what I think? Really? Bitch please explain. Please tell me what to think then Sassi!"

Eddie was yelling and waiting for a response, but I couldn't give him one.

Shaking his head, Eddie dropped the gun to the ground, got into his car and drove away.

After he was out of sight, I ran to the gun and put it in my purse.

What was he thinking?

Polo still screamed for Eddie and I didn't bother to turn around.

I just stood there until help arrived and pointed in the direction of the house.

What in the world have I done?

~***~

"My best friend Sassi! My fucking best friend! It could have been anyone else. Anyone other than Polo. Why Polo? Why Polo?"

Eddie was screaming at the top of his lungs and I was almost scared to answer him.

I'd walked all the way home the day before and when I got there Eddie and the kids were gone.

I called the daycare to see if they had been picked up.

They had.

I called Eddie over and over but he never answered the phone.

I stayed up all night long, calling, crying and texting him but he never said a word.

Polo called looking for him too but he was the last person that I wanted to talk to.

I wasn't sure what he'd said happened to him, but I was sure that he hadn't said that Eddie did it.

Finally, the next morning, Eddie walked in, ready for war.

"Why Sassi?"

"It happened so fast. I don't know why. I'm sorry. I was feeling a little unhappy. And it just happened. Our relationship was kind of boring, you didn't believe in my writing like I wanted you to, and the sex had been an issue before the pills, and it just happened. Polo was there and it just happened."

"It just happened? It happened because you wanted it to happen! And right under my nose. You were screwing my best friend right under my fucking nose! And here lately I had been giving you everything you asked me for so stop giving me excuses! Just say it out loud for me one time. Eddie, I fucked your best friend because I wanted to. Just say it!" Eddie just sounded so angry and distraught and I tried to plead with him but he wouldn't listen.

"Where are the kids?"

"Why?"

"What do you mean why Eddie? They are my kids too."

"Were you thinking about them when you were bouncing on their god father's dick? Huh? Were you thinking about them then?"

I cried harder and harder with every word that he said but he didn't stop.

He kept talking and calling me names and insulting my character.

Finally, he twisted off his wedding band and threw it in my face.

"No Eddie. No. Don't leave me. I love you."

"You love me? No. You don't love me."

"Yes I do. Yes I do. I'm sorry."

"If I could kill you and get away with it, I swear that I would. I swear I would make you maggot food, right here, right now! But our boys need at least one of their parents. They've already lost their loose booty mother. They can't lose their father too," Eddie said.

"Eddie, you are not taking my kids away from me."

"Watch me."

"You can't do that. They are my kids."

"They were your kids."

"No, please Eddie. Please, I'm sorry," I held on to him as he tried to leave.

"Don't leave me please."

"Get off of me Sassi! I hate you. I swear on everything that I love that I hate you!"

And with that, he pulled away from me and left me crying my eyes out as though I was some clingy one night stand or delusional side chick or something.

The next few minutes and even the next few days after that were an absolute blur.

I hadn't been to work.

I had barely eaten.

All I did was cry and the worst part of all was that I hadn't seen my kids.

Eddie wasn't even taking our oldest son to school and neither of them had been to daycare.

He couldn't do this.

He couldn't take my babies from me.

He hadn't come back to the house since that day or answered any of my calls.

I felt like I was going insane.

I ruined my life.

I ruined my marriage and my family.

What were Polo and I thinking?

I was the one that had everything to lose and I had lost it all.

And it was all his fault.

Depression was setting in and I had started to think a few things that I never thought would cross my mind.

I had been going through all of this on my own, and it was time that I told someone.

I needed someone to tell me that life was still worth living.

I needed someone to tell me that everything was going to be okay.

I headed to my phone and called my best friends.

I needed them.

Patrice was out of town as always, but Micki was there in less than five minutes.

"What happened to the one time Sassi?"

"I don't know. It was supposed to be but I couldn't help it. He'd shown up to dinner with Patrice and I guess it triggered something inside of me."

"What? Patrice?"

"Yeah and I think that I was really starting to fall for him too."

"Like what Sassi?"

"Like love. But it all went away once Eddie found out. I just want Eddie back. I just want my kids back."

"I told you to be careful. I told you. I knew something bad was going to come from this. I knew it. I could feel it. It was just too close to home Sassi. But he will forgive you. Eddie is a good guy and I believe that he will forgive you."

"I don't think so."

"Trust me. He will. He loves you so much Sassi. Everything is going to be fine."

I laid my head on her shoulder and I waited for her to say something else encouraging but she didn't.

Instead, she said something that took me by surprise.

"Besides, he has to forgive you; he isn't Mr. Innocent himself."

I lifted my head to look at her.

That's the second comment I've heard in regards to Eddie's faithfulness.

Or maybe I should say the lack there of.

"What?"

"I'm just saying."

"You're just saying what?"

"Maybe you should ask him if he has ever been unfaithful to you."

"Has he? How would you know that?"

Micki took a deep breath.

"I don't want to get in the middle of this."

"The middle of what? You knew that Eddie cheated on me and didn't say anything?"

"What was I supposed to say? You and Patrice are both of my friends," Micki said and covered her mouth.

What did she just say?

Patrice?

Patrice had been with Eddie and was trying to get with Polo too?

Maybe we were more like sister's than I'd thought.

But she'd been with Eddie?

Oh God…I'm going to kill her!

~***~

I had been calling Patrice's phone over and over again but she wasn't answering the phone.

Last we'd heard was that she was in Brazil, but her ass was mine as soon as she was back in the states.

Micki told me what she knew; at least what she'd wanted me to know that she knew.

I was sure that she was leaving out a few details.

According to what she'd said, Patrice and Eddie had fooled around a few times before I'd even met him.

And they continued to screw from time to time, after Eddie and I were an item, and possibly after we were married.

Maybe that's why Eddie always acted like he had some kind of problem with Patrice.

Maybe that's why he didn't want her around.

Oh, and there was more.

According to Micki, Patrice had gotten pregnant and Eddie made her get rid of the baby.

That bitch had gotten pregnant by my husband?

I couldn't even begin to explain what I was going to do to her.

After the abortion, they officially broke it off and hadn't dealt with each other since.

But that's only as far as Micki knew of.

But I was going to get to the bottom of it all.

I was going to get the truth even if I had to beat it out of one of them.

How could Patrice do that to me?

And Eddie?

Never would I have even guessed that he would step out on our marriage.

I had never had to question his loyalty.

Now I knew first-hand how Eddie felt after finding out about me and Polo.

And it wasn't a good feeling.

It was the worst feeling that I'd ever felt and somebody deserved to pay for my pain.

Eddie had no right to be mad at me for what I'd done because apparently he had done the same thing.

The only difference was that he hadn't gotten caught.

And I was the only one that didn't know about it.

Of course Polo knew; which he'd slipped up and mentioned it too.

And to find out that Micki knew and had been keeping it from me was more than disturbing and I didn't know whether to be mad at her or not.

She should have told me.

Damn it somebody should have told me!

She only said that she didn't want to be in the middle but at the end of the day that was a bunch of bull.

Eddie is my husband.

Not my boyfriend.

Not just my baby daddy.

But my damn husband!

Micki also said that Patrice said that it wasn't worth mentioning since it wasn't a big deal and just sex, but once they continued to fool around after we were married, Micki said that she'd warned her that one day it was all was going to blow up in her face and it finally did.

Patrice got pregnant and from what Micki said, she'd actually wanted to keep the baby.

But Eddie wouldn't let her.

He told her to get rid of it.

Her whole "I don't want a husband or kids" attitude was apparently a result of what Eddie had taken her through.

She'd even said that Patrice told Eddie that she would make up a baby daddy and raise the baby on her own but Micki said that Eddie told her that he would make her life a living hell if she went through with it.

Micki said that Patrice was so stressed out that she finally gave in, had the abortion and never looked back.

At least this was all of the things that Patrice had told her.

Had Patrice told me that they had sex before things got serious between us, I would have never even dated him.

Let alone married him.

Patrice and I had been friends for forever and I would never overstep a boundary like that, but she had.

She had done the unthinkable!

And I was going to catch a case!

She didn't answer my call, again, so I called Eddie for the thousandth time.

It had been a week and two days without seeing the kids and a week since I'd even talked to or seen Eddie.

This was ridiculous!

He still wasn't answering my calls.

I still didn't know where they were.

I'd gone to the police but since Eddie was their father and on their birth certificates, they instructed me to go in more of a domestic, courtroom battle direction.

I didn't want to hear that.

I just wanted to see my babies.

I just wanted my family back.

After a few more calls, finally, surprisingly, he picked up.

"You bastard! You had sex with Patrice!"

Eddie was quiet.

It took a minute but he finally spoke.

"What?"

"You had sex with Patrice! And you had the nerve to come at me about Polo? How dare you!"

"Who told you that?"

"What? All you have to say is who told me that?"

"Yes. Who told you that?"

"Micki. What does that matter?"

Surprisingly Eddie chuckled.

"Hmm, well did she tell you what she did?"

Oh hell.

What the hell did Micki do?

"What did she do?"

Eddie didn't answer my question.

"What did she do Eddie? So you did sleep with Patrice?"

"Only before you and I were married. It was never after you were my wife. It wasn't a big deal. Only a few times, and we agreed that it wasn't worth mentioning."

"Liar! You got her pregnant Eddie!"

"No I didn't Sassi. And as I said, I never, not once, broke our vows."

I didn't believe him.

He was lying.

And thinking back to Polo's small comment, I knew that Eddie had to be lying.

"You are the married slut, not me. You slept with my best friend Sassi. You broke our vows."

"And you slept with mine too Eddie!"

"We had a thing before you. Sex. Nothing more. Nothing less. And truth be told, Patrice isn't a friend to anyone. Hell, the only person she really cares about is herself and you know that. And despite what Micki may think that she knows, I never slept with Patrice once we were married Sassi."

He could save his lies.

I was heated!

But he sounded calm which pissed me off even more!

"What happened with Polo was you karma bitch!" I screamed at him.

Eddie didn't say anything.

I wanted him to feel how I felt at that moment, so I kept going.

"Did you cum in two minutes when you had sex with her too?" I growled.

Maybe that was a low blow but I no longer felt like shit.

He was just as bad as I was, and in my opinion, he had done worse.

Instead of answering my question, Eddie hung up.

I was so angry that I started to scream.

I screamed so loud and for so long that my throat felt as though it was being ripped into two.

My life was falling apart right in front of my eyes.

My husband was gone and had taken my kids.

Eddie and Patrice had sex before me and while I was with Eddie.

Not to mention that it had been said that he had gotten her pregnant.

And what was it that Micki hadn't told me?

This was all a bad dream.

I was about to lose my mind.

Just as I was about to fall out crying, Mama called.

She was the last person that I wanted to talk to, but I answered the phone anyway.

"What Mama?"

"I told you so."

"Yeah, let me guess, Eddie called you?"

"Yep."

"Did he tell you were he is with my kids?"

"Yep."

"Where are they?"

Mama didn't answer me.

"Why didn't you listen to me Sassi? You let Polo ruin your marriage. Was it worth it? Really was it worth it?"

"Mama, where is Eddie with my kids?"

"They were staying with me but they are gone now."

"Gone where?"

"I don't know Sassi."

"Why didn't you call and tell me Mama? Why didn't you tell me that they were there?"

"I been calling you for days but you always ignore my calls, even before you got caught. But you made this bed Sassi, and now you have to lay in it."

Mama hung up on me.

Why the hell was my Mama on his side?

She was *my* Mama!

Damn!

I immediately called Eddie's parents but his mother screamed in my ear and hung up.

He'd told everybody what I'd done.

But I bet none of them knew that he was guilty of the same damn crime.

I needed someone in my corner and since Micki's loyalty was up for question that only left one person.

Polo.

Polo was there in a matter of minutes.

"He slept with Patrice."

"I know."

"And no one thought to tell me that?"

"It wasn't my place Sassi."

Yeah, I bet it wasn't.

I found it crazy that Polo wouldn't have tried to tell me years ago being that he said that he'd always wanted me from Eddie.

"Was it before we were married Polo? Or while we were married?"

"I don't know Sassi."

"Yes you do! Your friendship with him is just as much as over as our marriage is so why not tell me?"

"Our friendship isn't over Sassi."

I stared at him.

"You talked to him?"

"Nope."

"Then how can you say that?"

"I just know."

They were close and all, but Polo was crazy if he thought that there wasn't going to be any consequences to what we'd done to Eddie.

He hated me.

And I was sure that he hated Polo just as much.

Hell, he'd already shot him, what more proof did Polo need?

"What are you going to do?"

I shook my head.

What kind of question was that?

Of course I had no idea what to do now.

I didn't know how to feel.

I didn't know what to say.

I didn't know whether to kill Patrice and Eddie, or accept it all because I had done the same.

The betrayal that I felt was unexplainable but I could only imagine that Eddie felt the same way too.

"Come here," Polo said and reached out to me.

I shook my head.

What was I even thinking inviting him over here?

"Maybe you should just go."

"No. You need me. I'm not going anywhere."

Polo limped towards the couch and made himself comfortable.

Propping his leg up, he waited for me to let down my guard.

I sat beside him.

"Do you know where Eddie is with the kids?"

"No."

"Where would he go? You know him best?"

"Your mother's," Polo responded.

Damn.

He really did know Eddie but Eddie had been to Mama's and gone.

I started to cry.

Polo held me close to him.

"It's going to be okay."

"No it's not and you know it."

"Run away with me."

I pulled away from him.

"No Polo. I want my family. I want my kids. And I know Eddie did something foul just like I did, but maybe we can get past this," I said to him.

"But you love me Sassi."

Before all of this, I'll admit, I felt like I was falling in love with him.

We were having sex all the time and sharing more personal, intimate, details with each other.

I hadn't seen him drunk in forever and he was giving me all of the things that I had been missing in my marriage.

But at the end of the day, he wasn't Eddie.

He wasn't my husband or the father of my kids, therefore, he could never be my forever.

"Polo, we messed up big time. And now we both have to make it right."

"I love Eddie like a brother, I really do. But I love you more Sassi. I don't want to lose what we have. I don't want to give this up. Even if that means that I have to give up Eddie."

Polo was crazy!

"I've lost everything behind you, this. No more Polo. No more."

"I'm not going anywhere Sassi. I'm not going anywhere."

"You don't have a choice Polo."

"See, that's where you are wrong…I do."

I stood up and gave Polo the evil eye.

He got my drift and stood up behind me and I followed behind him to the door.

"Eddie will take you back. I will remain his best friend. And once things are back to normal, we will pick things up where we left them off," Polo said and he waddled out the door and headed to his car.

He had never been the sharpest tool in the shed so I didn't even deem it necessary to comment to his ignorance.

Polo and I would never have sex again.

Polo and Eddie would probably never be friends again.

My feelings had never been clearer and with my priorities finally back in place and with my heart begging to be put back together again, I had to figure out how to get my husband back, and I knew just how to do it too.

****

CHAPTER 6

"Why have you been calling me like you are crazy?" Patrice said walking in my house, being that I had the front door open.

I'd called her a thousand times, but I'd never told her what I wanted.

I hadn't left it on her voicemail or sent a text.

I needed her to hear the words come out of my mouth.

Micki swore to stay out of it and that she wouldn't tell her anything if she talked to her before I did, and I was sure that from Patrice's statement, Micki or anyone else for that matter hadn't given her a heads up of what was going on.

I sat the groceries down that I had been holding.

Eddie and the boys hadn't stayed at home in over three weeks now, but finally I had seen them.

Eddie had been by plenty of times to get some of their things and he told me that he wasn't giving them back to me and that I would have to battle him in court for custody if that's what I wanted to do.

But we had met in public places so that I could see them.

He'd had some crazy papers signed by him and a lawyer saying that I was a threat to their well-being and that I couldn't take them from the school or the daycare.

But I hadn't even tried.

To be honest, I was such a mess that it was a good idea that Eddie had them.

I had to figure everything out and maybe that was the best place for them to be; with their father, wherever the hell that was.

But Eddie agreed to bring them to the house for the first time, and I was going to cook them all dinner.

Eddie and I were still in a bad place but I was going to win him back.

I was going to save my marriage.

I'd tried to forget what he'd done with Patrice but with her standing in my face, all I felt was rage.

"Why is this house such a mess? It's Saturday. Where is everyone?"

She walked closer to me and I glanced at the knife on the counter but decided to go old school and balled up my fists.

Without her expecting it, I threw the first blow.

But Patrice didn't hesitate to retaliate and we rumbled until we both finally gave up.

The groceries were all over the kitchen floor and both of us were in obvious pain.

"What the hell is wrong with you!"

Patrice was tending to her busted lip, while I sat trying to figure out whether my wrist was broken or not.

"You slept with my husband!"

Her eyes got as big as the bruise on her left cheek.

"Who told you that?"

She'd asked the same thing that Eddie asked as though secrets were meant to stay hidden forever.

Though I was hoping that mine would have stayed under wraps for as long as possible, things never tend to work out that way.

"There wasn't any point in telling you about us. It was before you and it was just sex."

"Just sex? And you didn't think that I needed to know that Patrice? And you had sex while we were married, so don't give me that before me bull crap!"

"No. The last time that Eddie and I had sex was about six months before you guys got married. We actually met to discuss whether we should tell you or not. Things got a little heated and it just sort of happened. But it never happened again after that. I swear."

I tried to lunge for her, but she moved from within my reach.

So Eddie hadn't broken our vows.

Still, he'd broken my heart.

"You were my best friend Patrice."

"Which is why I didn't think that you needed to know about Eddie and me. It was the past. You two hit it off. That one time, before you and Eddie got married, should have never even happened. And even before that night, I was already telling you that I just didn't think that he was a good fit for you but he made you happy and at the end of the day, that was all that mattered. I didn't want a few booty calls to ruin that for you."

She sounded sincere, which was different for her.

Patrice was so shady, conceited, and selfish that she rarely said anything that sounded like she had a heart, but at the moment, I could hear in her voice that she thought that not telling me about their relationship in the beginning was the right thing for her to do.

And as far as her sleeping with him while we were engaged, well, that was worth another ass whopping.

"You betrayed me. Our friendship for the past decade has been a lie."

"Sassi, I never meant to hurt you. The decisions that I made were always to keep from hurting you."

"So you got pregnant by Eddie and got rid of the baby not to hurt me Patrice? Or because he told you too?"

Patrice looked at me.

"The only person that could have told you that I was pregnant by Eddie is Micki, because she is the only person that I told that lie too. I wasn't pregnant by Eddie all of those years ago Sassi. I was pregnant by your father."

What?

I looked at her and almost threw up in my mouth.

"What a minute, you said that he molested you Patrice. That's what you told me and that's what I told Mama."

"I lied. I came on to him and he declined me, so I lied. I was too young then I suppose. Why do you think that I didn't want to press charges? I'd said that it was because of you, but really it was because things hadn't happened exactly how I'd told you. But a few years ago, right after Eddie and I did whatever that last time, I ran into your Dad at a bar. He was drinking as always. And one thing led to another and we fooled around for a while. I got pregnant by your Daddy Sassi. I told Micki that it was by Eddie since she knew that he and I had sex and because she had been the one to drive me to and from the abortion clinic. She didn't need to know the truth and she was never supposed to tell a soul so I didn't expect to have to ever explain this to anyone. I got rid of the baby because of you. Having a baby by your father was just too much, especially considering the lie that I'd told on him in the past."

That bitch!

Granted I wasn't my father's biggest fan before the alleged incident because he was a drunk, but after she'd said that he touched her, I absolutely hated him and I never forgave him.

I didn't let him come to my wedding or even be around his grandkids for that very reason and all along she'd lied?

Mama hated him, yet stayed with him, but hated him for his ways and what she'd thought that she'd done, yet Patrice had cried wolf?

I could kill her!

"Get the hell out of my house Patrice and I don't ever want to see you or talk to you again. Ever! Don't come back here. Don't call me. Don't speak when you see me. Just get out of my house and out of my life!"

Patrice looked at me, but she stood up.

I stood up, slowly as she stood there, looking at me.

"Sassi, I never meant to hurt you. I was coming to tell you that I met someone, in Brazil, and that I was moving there. So I will be out of your life for good just like you want. I guess this is goodbye."

I looked at her.

I was so angry at her that I started to cry.

She had been my friend since we were kids and I loved her so much.

I loved her like my own flesh and blood and I couldn't believe that she would hurt me this way.

She turned to leave and for some reason I called her name.

She stopped and I stood up and approached her.

I reached out my arms to her and for only a second we hugged.

I wanted to breakdown but I couldn't.

She had to go.

There was no way that we could rebuild after all of this.

I had to use everything that I had towards getting my marriage back on track and I just didn't have anything left to give to her.

We pulled away from each other and she headed out of the kitchen.

"Goodbye," we both said at the same time and I knew that I would never see her again.

And honestly, I didn't want to.

~***~

I hadn't heard from Polo and I couldn't understand why I missed him.

He hadn't bothered me.

He hadn't called me.

He hadn't come by the house to see how things were going between Eddie and I.

It was a good thing that he was staying away.

But still, if I had to be honest with myself, I could honestly say that I missed his presence.

But that wasn't important.

What was important was getting my husband to love me again.

I'd forgiven him for not telling me about Patrice and whatever it was that they'd done before we were married.

I just wanted him to forgive me and take me back.

Sure, we probably wouldn't have the perfect marriage but we never have.

And if things went back to normal, eventually, someday I might go back to feeling like he was the wrong husband again, but I didn't care about that.

I just wanted my family.

Things would never be right.

Things would never be perfect.

But what we had was ten times better than this.

And I had to get it back.

Just out of curiosity, I turned down Polo's street.

More than likely his cars were probably in the garage, so I wouldn't know if he was there or not, but I figured that I could still just ride by.

I wasn't planning to stop or anything.

I was just riding through.

I neared Polo's house and I had to blink twice at what I saw.

Polo and Eddie were leaned up against Eddie's car.

They appeared to be talking, or maybe even laughing but I took a quick right before either of them had a chance to notice me.

What?

Were they making up?

When?

How?

Eddie was still giving me such a hard time and yet he was over there cackling with Polo?

How did Polo know that would happen?

How did he know that Eddie would forgive him?

No.

I couldn't have seen what I thought I saw.

There just had to be some kind of explanation.

I almost became offended, but I had a better idea.

I turned my car around and sped to Polo's house.

I pulled up to see the Eddie's car was gone.

Polo was nowhere in sight either.

What the hell is going on here?

I called Eddie but of course he didn't answer.

I went out on a limb and called Polo too, but he didn't pick up either.

Parking my car, I went to ring Polo's doorbell.

And I almost started running once Eddie opened the door.

Damn. Damn. Damn.

"Sorry, but if you were coming for seconds, or seconds times a hundred, Polo isn't here."

Eddie's eyes were filled with disappointment.

"Actually I was coming to see if he had been able to get through to you. He's gone in your car?"

"If he isn't here, and you don't see my car, what do you think? And at the end of the day, Polo was a friend. You were my wife. A big damn difference Sassi. But Polo isn't here so I guess you shouldn't be here either. Would you like for me to tell him that you stopped by?"

Eddie was being sarcastic and I could tell that he was upset.

"No. Are you still bringing the kids by later?"

Eddie shrugged and I turned and headed back to the car.

I just keep making things worse.

He and the boys were coming by later, and I didn't want to piss him off any more than he already was, so it was best for me to just leave.

But I still wanted to know what it was that I'd actually saw.

I wanted to know why he would be willing to forgive Polo and not me?

What kind of mess is that?

Damn, they said that friends were forever, but what about me?

It just didn't seem fair, but nothing in life was fair these days.

I drove home and I sat there for a long while until Eddie texted me and told me that he was still coming by.

"Hey."

"Hey."

The kids hugged me and kissed me.

They missed being home with me.

I was sure of it.

They ran off to do whatever it is that they do and I took a seat on the couch.

"I'm cooking. You guys are welcome to stay."

Eddie sat across from me.

He looked at me long and hard.

I debated internally whether or not I wanted to ask him more about him and Polo making up.

After sitting in complete silence, finally, Eddie pulled out a few papers.

"What's that?"

He stared at me.

"Divorce papers."

My heart dropped.

I started to babble but Eddie held up his finger.

"I went to see Polo today to I asked him why. Out of all of the women that he has had, why did he have to have mine too? He told me that you came on to him."

"What? That's not true. He came on to me Eddie."

"I know. Because I know Polo. He's even slipped and said things out of the way while he was drunk. And I know him. I'm sure he made the first move."

I wanted to tell Eddie that Polo fakes being drunk and he probably was just saying it to get it off of his chest.

But I left it alone.

"But he also said that it only happened once. He said y'all met up on several occasions, but that the sex only happened once. Is that true Sassi?"

Oh how I wanted to lie and say yes but I couldn't.

I'd lied to him enough already.

"No Eddie. Polo lied. It happened more than once."

I guess this is what I deserved.

Hell I guess neither of us really deserved this marriage because neither of us had been honest in the beginning.

I guess a divorce was the best option for us.

But Eddie didn't reach me the divorce papers.

Instead, he tore them up.

"I know. Polo told me. I just wanted to see if you would lie about it. But you didn't. Look Sassi, Polo and I will never have the friendship that we once had. And you and I will never have the marriage that we used to have either. But the fact is, I love both of you. That's my brother. He's had my back so many times despite what you may think and what you may know about. Yeah I'm pissed off but I really feel like he's my brother. And you are my wife. Even though I dealt with Patrice before we were married one last time, when I took those vows, I meant them."

"What are you saying?"

"I'm saying that I'm hurt."

"I know."

"I'm saying that I hate you."

"I know you do Eddie."

"I'm saying that I choose you."

I accidentally smiled.

I wasn't sure if it was appropriate or not so I quickly asked a question.

"What do you mean? What about you and Polo?"

"That's just it. If I work it out with you, or at least try to, Polo has to go. I can't have both. I'll never trust the two of you alone or around each other again. We talked about it. We shared some memories and some laughs today. He will always be my brother. Always. But he's also my enemy too."

"What are you saying Eddie?"

"I'm saying that if you want this marriage, if you want us to try to fix it, then we have to get rid of Polo. We have to kill him."

Lord…Eddie done lost his damn mind!

~***~

I headed out for lunch and saw that Eddie was already there.

I was back at work, and Eddie said that he'd wanted to talk.

He'd given me back the kids, despite what he'd said but he hadn't come back home.

As for Polo, I hadn't heard a peep out of him, so I wasn't sure if he was even worth worrying about anymore.

I thought about him sometimes, but I had my feelings under control and I knew what was important.

"Hey."

Eddie didn't say hey back.

He started to talk but I cut him off.

"Were you really serious about killing Polo? That's crazy Eddie."

"No."

I let out a deep breath.

I knew that he had to be kidding.

"Well, what do you want to talk about?"

We stopped at the restaurant.

"My business hasn't been doing as well as I have led you to believe. It was at first, but things have slowed down tremendously, and I think I may have to let it go."

I looked at him.

I'd always thought that the business was doing fine.

"Really? Is it that bad?"

"Yeah, it is. I even have the IRS breathing down my neck for back taxes. After the success of the first year, I thought that money would keep coming in, abundantly, so I didn't exactly do what needed to be done, and it back fired. I'm an accountant, surely I thought that I had projected the numbers right, but I hadn't. Things have been so slow despite my long hours, hard work and attempts of finding new clients. Hell, sometimes I had to pull out of our savings to cover things. But you never noticed because I would find a way to put it back. Even if I had to ask Polo for the money."

Wow.

I guess maybe he was stressed to the maximum from work and now I was sure that had something to do with his sexual performance.

And the fact that he was keeping it from me probably made it worse.

"Well, you have to do what you have to do. You're going to go back to some big company again?"

"From the looks of it I won't have a choice."

"Well, are you coming home?"

Eddie shook his head.

"No. Actually, I went back and filed for the divorce after all Sassi. I don't make you happy, no matter how much I tried. I don't please you, how you want to be pleased and I think that for right now, this is for the best. I can't get the images of you and Polo out of my mind, having sex, and maybe I will never get over it, but I have to try. But I can't do it with you."

Eddie pulled out papers again.

This time, he handed them to me.

"Who knows, maybe Polo should have been the one to talk to you and marry you all along. He saw you first. Maybe I ruined your happily ever after. But believe me, both of you ruined mine."

I frowned.

"What about you and Polo? Will y'all remain friends?"

"I don't know Sassi. But that's all that you and I will be from this day forward."

Eddie got out of the car and opened my door.

Tears streamed down my face, but he wiped them away.

He didn't say anything and neither did I.

He hugged me and I could feel that he was happy to be free.

Or maybe he was just happy with the choice that he'd made to not force what doesn't fit.

"I love you Sassi. I always will, no matter what."

I believed him.

But if I said it back, I was sure that he wouldn't believe me.

"Eddie, what did you mean by that remark that you made about Micki? What did she do?"

Eddie cleared his throat.

"She is the one that told me about you and Polo."

What?

I waited for Eddie and the kids to leave before I called Micki.

"How could you?"

She automatically knew what I was talking about.

"Easy. I was trying to save you from yourself."

"I didn't need you to save me Micki."

"Oh, but you did. You just don't know it yet."

What the hell did she mean by that?

"No I didn't."

"Look, I never told you this but Polo gave me a loan, once."

What is she talking about?

"We exchanged numbers one day a long while ago at your house and we chatted a few times. Of course he was trying to talk me out of my panties, but I never liked Polo on that level. He was sexy, but I knew that he had a thing for you, so I figured that I might as well play it smart. I was going through some tough times with bills, and he offered to help me out, as a friend, if you could even call him that. He said that he didn't want anything in return. But every man says that. And in actuality, every man wants something. I shouldn't have taken the money from him, but at the time I was desperate."

I listened attentively.

"I told him that I would pay him back, but he told me not to worry about it. So I didn't. After a while, and because I knew that we weren't going anywhere, and because I'd started talking to someone else at the time, I stopped being friendly with Polo. If he called, I wouldn't answer. If he texted, I wouldn't respond. I learned real quick that Polo doesn't like rejection. He started to text smart comments as to say that I'd used him like everyone else did and I was every bitch from here to Mexico. He just got real nasty, but I never asked him to do anything for me. He offered. But it was as though he'd forgotten that part of the story."

Sounds about right.

I'd heard him say on several occasions that he was tired of being used.

Mostly by his folks but I'd heard him say it in regards to women a few times too.

There was even a time, with his last wife, that he'd pretended to be broke or average, until after they were married.

He'd said that he'd wanted to be sure that she loved him for him and not the money.

He'd rented a small apartment and everything.

She married him, but she was a whore.

She couldn't seem to keep her legs closed, no matter how much money Polo had.

Karma.

"After a while, all of these strange things started to happen. The kid's dog turned up dead. Someone had stabbed him and laid him right on the front porch, with the knife still in his chest, for the kids and me to see. Just sickening. And then my tires were mysteriously coming up flat once a week. At first I thought that it was my new neighbor's weird ass kid that had just moved in. You remember me mentioning him?"

I nodded.

"Yeah. But then I talked to him one day and found out that he wasn't weird at all. He was just expressive with the way that he dressed. But things still kept happening. I went about two weeks without any mail. I had things getting turned off and when I called about them, they'd said that they had sent a notice but for some reason my mail was always missing. And then the time that my police raided my house for drugs, I knew that something crazy was going on. The police said that they'd received an anonymous tip. Tip my ass."

Interesting, something similar had happened to me.

The only catch was that drugs had actually ended up in my purse, which made me think that the police officer might have been called to the grocery store just for me.

At that point in time I had been ignoring Polo too, so if he was behind all of the things that had happened to Micki, because of rejection, he'd probably tried to get something to happen to me too.

He'd probably paid that girl to bump me and put something in my purse.

That's if Polo was behind it all.

"And then one day, it all just stopped."

"Why didn't you say anything?"

"Because you would have told Eddie. Eddie would have told Polo and I didn't want him to know that I knew that it was him. But I was positive that it was Polo. It all started happening right after he gave me the money and right after I started ignoring him. It had to be him," Micki said.

"That doesn't mean that Polo was responsible for those things."

Micki laughed wickedly.

"I know for a fact that he was. Polo is possessive. Polo is irrational and irresponsible. Polo is crazy," Micki said.

He hates to be called crazy.

But I'd always said that he was a little off.

But still, I didn't know what to think about what Micki was saying.

"You were headed for trouble Sassi. I had to stop you. Polo is trouble. I might have a few kids and I might didn't go to college like the rest of you, but I can see straight through Polo. And I don't like what I see. Work on you and Eddie and just leave Polo alone on that level. You sampled the goods, now go on."

Micki hung up before I could say anything else.

I pressed on her name to call her back, but immediately, I hung up the call.

I didn't appreciate what she had done.

Not one bit.

But if what she was saying was true and if she knew for a fact that Polo had been the one doing those crazy things to her, than I could kind of see her reasoning.

Maybe I should be thanking her for being messy instead.

~***~

Things were tight!

And Eddie's past had caught up to us.

Not only did Eddie have to let his business go, but the IRS had come in and taken everything that they could.

I only still had my car because it was in mama's name because I had bought it from her, cash, pretty much brand new, when she couldn't get out of the contract, but decided that she preferred a smaller car instead.

Thank goodness that we had been too lazy to actually get everything switched over because the IRS would have snatched it up too.

We'd lost the house, Eddie lost his car and they went in and took our savings.

I still had a small stash of mad money that even Eddie hadn't known about, so I had been able to use it during these hard time.

I'd down-sized to a two bedroom townhome.

And the rent there was just as much as a mortgage but I tried not to complain.

Things would be back to normal soon.

With the kids and with Eddie not working or living with us, things were always chaotic, and since everything was now on me financial, I was so overwhelmed.

But things could be worse.

Time was flying by and it was almost Christmas.

Eddie or his parents watched the boys while I worked, but even though that did save money, it wasn't enough.

My little savings had been gone and I was living from paycheck to paycheck and I didn't like it.

Not one bit.

I could see how eager and stressed out Eddie was trying to find a job, but he hadn't found one as of yet.

Eddie was so desperate that he would take anything.

But nothing had become available as of yet.

And things were harder than they had ever been before.

"Are you watching them here today?"

"Yeah."

Though Eddie stayed with his parents, it was easier for him to watch the kids at my place sometimes.

I headed out to work as Eddie continued to get our oldest son ready for school.

I had been working over every day just to make ends meet.

I clocked into work all of ten minutes late and just as I got settled at my desk, my boss motioned for me to come into his office.

"Sassi, I don't really know how to say this. But we're going to have to let you go?"

"What? No."

"Your job performance hasn't been what we need lately. And that's not including the leaving early, coming late, and the missing one day a week at least twice a month. Everyone is complaining and from a business perspective we are lacking."

"You know that I am going through a divorce and the IRS snatched everything that they could, so things have been tight. Things have been rough. But I'm good at this job and you know I can do the work. I promise I won't miss any more days and to be here on time."

"I'm sorry Sassi. But it's too late. I need your badge please."

I needed my job!

With Eddie out of work, I couldn't afford to be out of work too.

"Please."

He reached his hand in my direction.

I stood up and damn near threw my badge in his face.

How inconsiderate!

He knew that I was going through hell and he knew that I needed the money but he was firing me anyway.

I was already so stressed out and this was the icing on the cake.

Something just took over me.

I started knocking over everything on his desk.

I kicked over the chair that I had been sitting in and even pulled down the blinds from the big, glass windows surrounding his office.

I was in a rage as I ranted on and on, as everyone watched me as though I was some kind of crazy lady.

It wasn't until the security for the building walked in my direction that reality kicked in and I realized that I had gone too far.

And as the security led me outside, and the police pulled up, I knew then that I had definitely crossed the line.

I was going to jail.

Hours later, the cell door opened and I headed to sign some papers.

Mama was there waiting for me.

I'd called Micki to come bail me out and she must have called Mama.

Knowing her she probably didn't have a sitter or the money to even post my bail.

"I don't want to hear it Mama," I said immediately as I stared at her judgmental facial expression.

"I haven't said a word...yet."

Really I just didn't want to hear anything that she had to say.

We got into her car and just as soon as we started driving, she started talking.

"Sassi, you should have known that no good would have come from what you did. You brought this hell on yourself from screwing your husband's best friend, and I don't feel sorry for you."

"I didn't ask you to feel sorry for me Mama. I lost my job. I lost my husband. I lost my house. And today, I think I lost my mind. So forgive me, but I don't care what you think or what you feel about my situation. I already feel bad enough as it is."

"You and the kids can come live with me."

"I'd rather be homeless. I would live on the street first Mama before I came to live with you just to be reminded of what I did wrong every single day."

We pulled up at my townhomes and for some reason I couldn't open the door.

"Something is wrong with it. I'll have to get out and open it from the outside," Mama said.

I tried to roll down the window, but that didn't work either.

"Sassi, I know you think that I'm being hard on you, I just never wanted to see you going through the things that I had to go through. I didn't want you to make the same mistakes that I made."

I looked at her.

"I left my husband for your father. Well actually, my husband left me. But I'd wanted him to. I'd met your father and fell for him, although I was married. I'd been married for years before I met him, and if I could turn back the hands of time, I would. Other than having you and your brother, getting involved with your father was the worst decision that I have ever made. We fooled around for a few months, and I fell head over heels in love with him. He was perfect, though it seemed, and I preferred him over my husband who was everything that I didn't even know I needed at the time."

She took a deep breath.

I never even knew that Mama had been married before Daddy and no one had ever bothered to mention it either.

"I stopped coming home. I didn't care if he found out. And then finally he got tired and left me. As soon as he was gone, he filed for divorce and as soon as it was final, I moved your Daddy right on into the house that my husband had bought for me. The house that he'd offered to let me have so that he didn't have to be reminded of me. Anyway, I was sure that your father was the one. I was sure that I'd made a mistake and married the wrong husband and that I should have waited and married your father instead. But I was wrong. It wasn't until your father and I married that I saw his true colors and as you know, my life and our marriage was a waste since the day that we'd said "I do". I regretted my decision for years and that was part of the reason that I stayed with your father and never left. I made my bed, so I had to lay in it. So you see, I was trying to stop you Sassi from becoming me. I was trying to stop you from ending up like me."

Mama was almost in tears, but I'd beat her to the punch.

I was bawling and I knew at that moment, I should have listened to her.

I'd ruined every good thing that I had.

I'd even ruined Eddie, although he wasn't as innocent in all of this as I'd wanted him to be.

Just then I remembered Patrice's confession.

"Mama, Patrice lied about Daddy."

Mama looked at me.

"He never touched her inappropriately. He never molested her. She'd wanted him to touch her that day, and he'd turned her down. So she lied. The whole thing had been a lie. She confessed it to me."

I could have filled her in on the rest of it, but what was the point?

Daddy was dead and gone and Patrice was thousands of miles away.

We would never see either of them again, so I didn't need to tell her the whole truth just the part of the truth that actually mattered.

Mama exhaled and then got out of the car.

She walked around to the passenger side and opened it.

I hugged her as soon as I was on my feet and told her that I loved her.

She was only trying to protect me and I was thankful that she'd cared enough to give an effort, though I had messed everything up anyway.

It was too early for the oldest to be out of school, but seeing Eddie's car, I knew that he and our youngest boy was inside.

I walked in to find them napping on the couch.

I smiled at them.

I tip-toed over to them, and at the last second, I decided not to wake Eddie.

His phone vibrated on the table and though I wasn't intending to look at it, I did, just to see who was calling.

It was Polo.

We hadn't spoken in forever and I was doing my best to keep it that way.

He was part to blame for all of this and with the way that my life had been lately I wished that we could take it all back.

But we couldn't.

He stopped calling and then he sent a text.

Bro, I was just checking on you. I wanted you to know that I'm getting married. You're the only friend that I ever had, and I wanted you to be my best man. It all may be too much to ask but, I thought to give it a try.

Polo was getting married?

To who?

I reread the text, three times just to make sure that I had read it correctly.

Who in the hell was Polo marrying this time?

For some reason, I felt some type of way.

It wasn't anything sexual; it was more like anger.

He had ruined our marriage and now he thought that he had a right to get married?

Oh no, I don't think so.

After reading all of Polo's other messages that Eddie had ignored, I erased the message telling Eddie the big news and deleted the call from his call log.

Being that Mama hadn't taken me by my old job to get my car I stepped outside to call Micki and asked her for a ride.

I hardly spoke at all as she talked and once I reached my car, I headed in Polo's direction.

He wasn't getting a happily ever after if I couldn't have mine too.

What kind of mess was that?

I arrived at his house and knocked on his front door.

He opened it with a look of surprise on his face.

"Hey baby…did you miss me?" I said.

****

CHAPTER 7

Polo called over and over and I simply stared at the phone without answering it.

I'd shown up at his house with intentions to ruin his life the same way that he'd ruined mine.

He didn't have the right to get married.

He didn't have the right to be happy.

And I was going to make sure that he wasn't.

But as soon as I saw him, I changed my mind.

I tried to walk away, without saying a word, but Polo chased after me.

"What are you doing here Sassi?"

"Nothing. Never mind."

"I miss you."

"I bet."

"Why are you here?"

"I shouldn't have come here. This was a mistake."

"I've been trying to stay away. I'm trying to move on and get over my feelings for you. I even decided to marry a woman that I have been getting down with for over a year now. The woman that approached you about the video tape, remember? That's who I decided to marry."

Why was he lying?

That woman was dead.

I'd seen it on the news that she was in a hit and run so why was Polo saying that they were getting married?

I was sure that he knew that she had passed away.

And looking at him, I wasn't so sure that he wasn't responsible for it.

But why would he be lying about who he was getting married to?

Or was he simply lying about getting married all together?

And why would he lie on the dead woman of all people?

Just sick.

"I miss how things used to be. If I get married, things might go back to normal," Polo said.

"Eddie and I are about to finalize our divorce so I doubt it."

"Trust me, he won't finalize it."

"Why do you think that? He's serious Polo. We hurt him. He doesn't want to be with me, and are you guys even still friends like you hoped to be?

"We're working on it. I asked him to be my best man. If I get married, everything will be better."

"Polo, that woman that you just said that you were marrying is dead. I saw her on the news."

I didn't feel like playing games with him.

I didn't even know why I was still there talking to him.

But I had learned that with crazy folks, you had to confront them head on.

"So you saw the news huh?"

"No shit Sherlock. So what huh? Are you lying about who you are marrying? Or were you lying about getting married altogether?"

"No. I'm getting married…to somebody. I know that will make everything better."

Polo started to smile at me but I was so creeped out all of a sudden.

Maybe Micki was right about him.

It was more than just a few screws loose with Polo; he might need some serious help.

"Look Sassi, I couldn't be more messed up if I tried but I'm getting myself together. I am going to get married, soon. I'm going to try to stay married this time and try to live that lifestyle again. Oh, and I stopped drinking, completely."

I opened my car door.

I didn't congratulate him.

I just wanted to get away from him.

He grabbed the car door.

"I've been trying to let you be. I know that I ruined your life and I'm sorry. You were right, we made a big mistake."

"I told you Polo. But we can't change what we did."

"And I don't want to."

"I bet you don't."

"Sassi are you okay?"

I looked at Polo.

"No."

"Can I help in anyway?"

"No. Believe me. You have done enough."

I left right after my statement that day, but since then he had been calling like crazy.

I didn't understand why though.

Polo was one of those folks that if you give the an inch, they try to take a whole mile.

"Are you going to answer that?" Eddie asked.

"Nope."

He didn't say anything.

"Have you talked to Polo? If you don't mind me asking."

"I do mind you asking Sassi. I don't want to ever discuss anything with or about Polo with you. Ever."

I blinked twice to keep from rolling my eyes.

He didn't have to say all of that.

Eddie changed the subject.

"I got a job."

I smiled at him.

At least one of us needed one.

"Senior accountant. $250,000 a year. Benefits and a sign on bonus. You and the kids can have the bonus. I can go without until I get my first check."

Eddie handed me a $5000 check.

He didn't have to do it but he did.

I really messed up didn't I?

"We need to come up with a set amount to give to you for the kids every week or every month."

I stared at Eddie.

He was just as stubborn as an ox.

We had both been going through hell but he had to miss being a family.

I know I did.

"That's good. I'm so happy for you."

I stood up and hugged him.

We lingered for a second too long and I looked at him.

"I don't want to finalize the divorce Eddie."

Eddie didn't say anything.

"Let's start over."

Eddie took a breath.

"I don't know what the future holds. But I do know that we have to end in order to start over again."

He was sticking to it so I didn't press the issue.

A knock at the door caused us both to look in that direction.

I headed for it, and Eddie followed.

"Hey baby, why didn't you answer you phone?" Polo said as soon as I opened the door.

I heard Eddie huff and puff behind me.

I frowned at Polo and just as I was about to say something, he spoke again.

"Oh, so you finally told Eddie?"

I looked at him confused.

"Told me what?"

"Look Eddie, we both love you but we love each other too. We hope that you can understand."

"What!"

I screamed and Eddie pushed me out of the way.

"I wouldn't try anything stupid this time Eddie," Polo warned him, knowing that Eddie was about ready to swing on him.

"Eddie, I don't know what he's talking about."

"You weren't saying that when you stopped by on Tuesday, the day after you had gotten out of jail."

"Jail? When did you go to jail?"

"It's a long story," I said to Eddie.

I had only told him that I had gotten fired.

I didn't fill him in on the destruction of property charge that I had gotten too.

"You told Polo and didn't tell me?"

"I didn't tell Polo. I don't know how he knows."

"Really Sassi, let's be honest. We don't have to lie anymore. Eddie deserves to know the truth. We've lied to him enough. She came and asked to borrow money and we talked about us. She said you were having hard times. Why didn't you come to me? You know I would have helped you."

Eddie looked as though he was about to get a life sentence.

"I don't need your help Polo. I didn't need it in my bedroom, and I don't need it now."

Eddie looked at me.

"He's lying Eddie."

Eddie shook his head and walked outside.

Polo put his hand in his pocket as Eddie passed by him.

Did he have a gun?

Eddie got into his mother's Mercedes that he had been driving and sped away.

Polo looked at me and as soon as he did, I smacked him with everything I had in me.

"Why would you come here? How do you even know where I live? Why would you say that?"

Polo grinned.

"If I can't have you, neither can he. And I will make sure of that," he said and he walked away too.

~***~

"Move Polo, I have a job interview and I'm going to be late."

Polo had his car parked directly behind mine.

The kids had stayed with Eddie at his parent's the night before so that his parents could watch them that day.

After searching for what seemed like forever, I had finally gotten a call back.

It seemed as though Polo was riding by every day and some days he even had the nerve to stop and knock on the door.

He wasn't at all sorry about lying to Eddie, and I could tell that he was going to make it his business to see to it that Eddie and I didn't get back together.

Eddie didn't know what to believe and he wouldn't even talk about what Polo said to him that day.

He didn't want to hear anything that I had to say.

He didn't want to discuss anything that had to do with me or Polo.

The divorce was finalized and for the most part, I was a free woman.

But I didn't want to be free.

I wanted to be with Eddie.

"Polo move."

"What is the job paying? I'll pay you the same salary. All you have to do is work for me."

"Work for you? Doing what?"

"You know what I like."

Nasty bastard!

"You will never touch this again."

"Is that right?" Polo smiled.

"Can you please move so I can go to my interview?"

"I'll take you. I want to talk to you anyway."

"Hell no."

"Oh, well then."

Polo just sat there as I checked the time on my phone.

Ugh!

He was such an asshole.

Maybe I should take some kind of restraining order out on him or something.

That would keep his ass away from me.

"Whatever Polo."

I pouted and headed to his car.

"Where are we going?"

"5th street."

"I heard that you and Eddie are officially divorced."

"You seem to hear everything."

"I know a lot of people. So are you?"

"Yes. We are."

"So you're free to do what you want to do?"

I looked at him.

"No Polo. Don't even think about it. My life is the way it is because of you."

"I'm telling you. I can make you happy."

"After the crap that you pulled in front of Eddie, I wish I would."

"It's all because I love you."

"What happened to you getting married to the dead woman?" I asked his lying ass sarcastically.

"I was going to find somebody to marry so that things could go back to how they used to be."

"Did you kill that girl Polo?"

"No. Why would you ask me that?"

"No reason."

"I want you."

"Too bad. It's right here."

Polo stopped in front of the building and I got out.

I shook off any bad energy that may have been surrounding me and I headed inside.

Only thirty minutes later, I was headed back out and Polo pulled up to the curb so I could get inside of the car.

"Did you get it?"

"Nope."

I was so disappointed.

I needed a job.

Eddie was back working but we weren't together and though he was going to give me money for the kids, I needed my own money.

I was sure that he would make sure that my bills were paid if I needed him to, with the kids being in the house and all but eventually, I was going to have to stand on my own two feet.

What if he started to date again?

He would surely get funny with his money.

I didn't even want to think about Eddie being with another woman.

As far as I was concerned, he still belonged to me.

Even if he did pretty much hate me.

"You will get the next one. I know a few people. I can make some calls."

I looked at Polo.

"I'm serious. You will be surprise the type of people that are secretly apart of the sex toy industry. Everyone knows that sex sells, and everyone who is anyone wants a piece of the pie. I can make some calls for you."

"No thanks Polo."

"Well, why not finish your book? I'm sure our little situation would be plenty of inspiration."

He was right.

It would be.

I hadn't tried to write anything in a while.

I was always feeling down or stressed out.

"Maybe."

"Can I at least take you out to brunch?"

"Polo, just take me home."

"Look Sassi, I'm not going to do anything to you. Let me just take you out. It's a free meal. I'll be on my best behavior. I promise."

I rolled my eyes and my stomach rolled *hers* too.

I was hungry as hell so brunch did sound pretty good.

"Okay Polo. But after that, take me straight home. I need to do some more job applications."

He nodded and we stopped at a small bistro.

Polo and I went inside and it was and I cringed at the sight of Eddie and the white lady waiting in line.

They were really close and Eddie was flashing his million dollar smile.

"Eddie?"

He turned around to face me.

He looked back and forth from Polo to me and then at the lady that he was standing with.

I stared at the woman who grinned at me.

"Hey I'm Shelly."

"I'm Sassi. Eddie's wife."

She swallowed.

"My ex-wife," Eddie added.

"Ex-wife? Eddie I thought you had never been married."

"Oh really Eddie? You were never married?"

He didn't say anything.

"You don't hear me talking to you? You were never married to me for almost nine years Eddie? Or with me for the past eleven years? Oh, and did you at least include that you had kids?"

"Kids? You told me that you didn't have kids."

Looks like Eddie hadn't claimed any of us.

Polo stood there and didn't say a word.

And neither did Eddie.

"I'm sorry. Who are you?"

"I'm Shelly. I told you that already. Or do you mean who am I to Eddie? Oh, we just work together. And I thought we, well, that doesn't really matter."

Eddie still said nothing and she waited for him to comment but he didn't.

"Why didn't you tell her that you were married or had kids Eddie?"

He still said nothing.

She got her food and headed towards the door, and Eddie followed behind her, still saying nothing.

What the hell was that?

I was mad!

And I do mean M-A-D!

"Polo I want to go."

"Okay."

Once we were in the car I turned to him.

"Who is she Polo?"

"I swear I don't know her. She probably is from his new job."

I studied him.

He was telling the truth.

"Why would he lie about us?"

"I don't know Sassi. I'm sure he has a good reason."

Polo started to drive and I couldn't think of one good reason why Eddie would say that he had never been married or didn't have kids.

Something just seemed off.

Polo pulled up at my house and I sat there.

Here I was still trying to figure out how to make things right with Eddie and he was off pretending as though I didn't even exist.

Hell, he wasn't even claiming our kids.

Had I hurt him that bad?

Had I made it to where he wanted to pretend that he hadn't spent the last decade with me?

I was insulted.

My feelings were definitely hurt.

"It will be okay Sassi."

I'd forgotten that Polo was there.

He touched my hand.

I didn't feel what I used to feel when he touched me but I was feeling something that I couldn't really explain.

He seemed to be the only one around me that actually wanted me or that even really seemed to care about me.

Maybe he was part the blame for everything but at least he still cared.

And at that moment, and after finding out that Eddie was lying about my existence to a woman that he was obviously interested in, more than anything else, I wanted to feel desired.

I opened the car door.

Polo didn't say anything.

He just looked concerned.

I wondered what was on his mind but I couldn't tell.

I stepped out of the car and just before I closed the door, I bent down to look at him.

"Come on," I said.

After a second or two…Polo got the hint.

****

CHAPTER 8

"Oh no," I mumbled.

I didn't even want to speak on it; I just had to come up with a plan.

I waited for Eddie to come into the house with the boys.

"They have already eaten. They just need baths and they should knock right out. I can stick around and give them one."

Eddie admitted to denying that he had an ex-wife and kids.

He said that he wasn't comfortable with telling people that he was divorced yet and that he and the woman had been becoming quite friendly.

But I was determined to mess all that shit up.

I asked him how he was going to explain it to her if they had ever truly started to date.

All he said was that he hadn't thought that far ahead.

I wished that I had at least talked to him about it first, instead of acting on my feelings and having sex with Polo.

I did it because I was angry and even though it was good, I knew that it was the wrong thing to do.

They weren't really friends anymore and I wasn't married, so I guess it wasn't as bad as it had been previously, but I was sure that Eddie wouldn't appreciate it.

But having just looked at my calendar before Eddie walked in, it appeared as though I had sex with Polo on one of my ovulation days.

I wasn't on birth control, and my tubes weren't tied.

And though we'd had sex with a condom, it broke during the 101 positions that Polo had put me in and we didn't notice it until the end.

At least I didn't.

I'm sure that he did.

I hadn't been pregnant since our youngest son strictly by keeping up with my ovulation and my most fertile days.

It doesn't work for everyone, but it had been working for me for years.

If I was ovulating or fertile and Eddie wanted sex, he would either wait, or wear a condom on those days.

And it had worked for us.

But I made a mistake.

I wasn't planning on having sex with Polo that day, or anybody else for that matter, so I hadn't been keeping up with it.

And I had a feeling that I might have made the biggest mistake of all.

It was too late for the morning after pill, so now I had to do something scandalous.

I had to find a way to make Eddie have sex with me.

I be damned if I had a baby by Polo and if I did, he would never know it.

Having sex with Eddie would be only a couple of days away from when I'd had sex with Polo, and I needed to make this happen between Eddie and I.

Someway.

Somehow.

Because with my bad luck lately, I had to make sure that I was two steps ahead of the problem, and if I turned up pregnant and wanted to pin it on Eddie, I at least had to make sure that he had gotten the goods.

"You never told me what you were doing with Polo that day?"

"He took me to an interview. I was having car trouble and he drove by. I was running late so he took me and called a tow truck to get my car home. After I didn't get the job, he offered me lunch. That was it."

Eddie looked at me.

"Oh."

"I will never ever deal with Polo, again. You never have to worry about that."

"If you did, that's your business Sassi."

"I wouldn't. He's your friend."

"That hadn't stopped you the first time. And we aren't friends anymore Sassi. When I divorced you, I divorced him too in a way."

Polo hadn't told me of any recent conversations of him and Eddie but I assumed that was how he had heard about the divorce.

From Eddie.

"You want me to bathe them right quick?"

I walked closer to him.

I wrapped my arms around him.

"Losing you was the biggest mistake I have ever made. I never meant to hurt you. I loved you so much and I still do."

"Move Sassi," Eddie said.

"I love you Eddie. And I miss you so much. I'm so sorry."

"Okay. It's the past. I'm just trying to go forward. Oh, did you need any money?"

He kept trying to change the subject as he tried to pry my fingers away from his neck.

"I love you so much. Do you still love me?"

Eddie looked irritated.

"Do you Eddie?"

He didn't say anything.

I tried to kiss him but he turned his head.

I took one of my hands and headed down to his *jimmy*.

It wasn't on hard like it used to be when I touched him.

But I was going to work on it.

"Kiss me Eddie."

"No."

"Why?"

"Why would I?"

Ouch.

"Because you love me."

Eddie looked at me as if he was saying so what, I love my mama too.

As though his love for me no longer meant anything to him.

I gave up and Eddie headed upstairs to give the boys a bath.

He really didn't want me.

I guess if some kind of pregnancy situation came up, I could go get it taken care of.

And Micki obviously knew a place since she had gone with Patrice to get rid of my brother or sister.

I could use some of the money that Eddie gave me because he always gave me more than enough.

So, I guess sex with Eddie wasn't the only option.

After a while, I headed upstairs to see the kids bonding with their father so I left them alone.

He was still an amazing dad even though he wasn't home with us every night.

That was all that really mattered.

I got comfortable and laid across the bed and entertained my thoughts.

Sometime or another I must have dozed off.

"They're asleep. I'm about to go."

I just looked at him but I didn't say anything.

He just stood there and finally I turned my head.

I was only wearing a t-shirt and though I couldn't see him I got the feeling that he was looking at my bare ass.

I wondered if he had been with anyone.

Considering his little problem, he probably hadn't.

After a while I heard his footsteps come closer and closer.

Everything was still for a while, quiet and then out of nowhere, he grabbed a hand full of my hair.

Hard.

"Eddie, ouch!"

"Shut up."

He turned me flat on my stomach and I heard him undo his pants.

He motioned for me to get on my knees and once I was, it wasn't long before I felt Eddie inside of me.

Eddie started to stroke and I waited for him to cum but he didn't.

He kept going.

He kept pumping and after a while, I started to get into it.

It felt different.

It felt better.

He grunted and rammed his cock inside of me, angrily, as though he was trying to hurt me or something.

As though he was trying to make me bleed.

But I actually liked it so I cooed.

Why did sex have to be like this after we'd divorced?

He hadn't even taken a pill and he was lasting long enough to remind me of why I'd married him in the first place.

"Oh, I'm about to cum. I'm about to cum."

I felt Eddie start to release, but I was right behind him.

"Yes! Yes Polo. Yes!"

Wait a minute…who?

I couldn't even concentrate on the explosive orgasm that I had just gotten because I knew that I had just called Eddie Polo's name.

Maybe he hadn't noticed.

Eddie got up, put on his pants and called me a bitch.

Uh oh…yes he did.

What the hell Sassi!

He stormed out of my bedroom and down the stairs.

He yelled bitch one last time and then slammed the door behind him.

If he didn't hate me before he damn sure hated me now.

There wasn't a chance in hell that he would ever take me back.

Entering the bathroom and wiping the aftermath between my legs, I knew that I was going to have to apologize.

But at least I got his sperm.

~***~

"I miss you."

To be honest I missed Micki too.

I guess I couldn't be mad at her; after all she hadn't really done anything, except run her mouth, as always.

"I miss you too girl," I said.

She sat across from me.

"Have you talked to Patrice?"

Micki looked uncomfortable by the question.

"Yeah."

"She told you what happened between us?"

"Yeah."

"She still in Brazil?"

Micki was hesitant.

"No."

"Where is she?"

"She's back here."

"Why? I thought she was moving to Brazil."

"She changed her mind about staying I guess."

I could tell that Micki didn't want to talk about Patrice.

Maybe she didn't want to feel torn or obligated to say much so I let the subject go.

And she was more than happy to change the subject.

"So, how do we get you and Eddie back together?"

I shook my head.

"He don't want me girl."

"Why not?"

I hadn't girl talked with her in a while, and though I was sure that she wasn't going to be too happy with what I had to tell her, I was going to tell her anyway.

"I called Eddie Polo's name during sex."

"You didn't."

I shook my head up and down.

"How could you do that? How did that happen?"

"I don't know. He was killing it from the back and had me screaming and all kinds of stuff. And the wrong name came out.

Micki shook her head.

"Well, he ain't gonna take you back now."

"That's what I said."

Micki's phone started to ring and she looked at it but didn't answer it.

I leaned over to see that it was Patrice.

"Answer it."

"No. I will call her back."

"Answer it."

Micki rolled her eyes.

I stared at her and finally she smacked her lips and answered the phone.

"Hello?"

I couldn't hear what Patrice was saying but Micki listened to her for a little while.

"Yeah. I'm with Sassi right now."

Micki listened for a long while again.

"Okay."

Micki hung up the phone.

"What did she say?"

"Nothing."

Micki was definitely hiding something and it was killing her to hold it in.

She grabbed her purse and stood up.

"I gotta go."

I was sure that it was something to do with Patrice but she went on her way and I was left alone.

One day she would break down and tell me whatever it was.

I was sure of it.

I headed back to take a seat..

I was so bored and I was tired of sitting around the house with nothing to do.

I was ready to go back to work.

The kids were staying overnight with Eddie at his parents, so I was going to die of boredom all day and night if I didn't find something to get in to.

I wasn't ready to start dating yet, even though I was probably going to have to get ready sooner or later.

Eddie wouldn't even come in the house since I'd called him Polo's name during sex.

He now made me bring the kids outside.

Speaking of Polo, I hadn't really heard from him.

He hadn't been as worrisome as I thought that he would be after screwing him, so I could only assume that he was doing other things or other women too.

But that was okay with me.

I headed to get my laptop and decided that writing would be the perfect way to pass time.

I reread some of my writing and then opened up a new document.

I had a better story to tell.

My own.

I thought of a title and then it came to me.

"The Wrong Husband"

Yeah.

I could definitely write one hell of a story about that.

~***~

"I need you to ride with me," Micki said.

"Where?"

"Just come on. And you don't need to bring the kids."

Eddie was at work but I called his mother to ask if she could get them for me.

She acted like she hated me too, but she didn't mind watching her grandkids.

We dropped off the kids and then Micki drove for a while.

She was silent for most of the ride and then we came to a stop.

It was a house; well a business that looked like a house.

Immediately I noticed that it was some kind of lawyer's office.

"What are we doing here?"

Micki didn't answer me, so I followed her inside.

She spoke to the receptionist and then had a seat beside me.

"What's this about Micki?"

"You will see."

After a few minutes, we were led to a back room and we took a seat at a big round table.

An old white man finally came in the room and sat in front of us.

"Good evening ladies. Let's get started."

"Wait. Could someone tell me what's going on here?"

"I'm sorry. You don't know?"

"Know what?"

"Patrice died Sassi," Micki said.

My heart sank into the pit of my stomach.

"What? When? How?"

"She had a brain tumor. She had it for years, which is why she had been traveling like a crazy woman."

I shook my head.

"Why didn't anyone tell me?"

"No one knew. She just told me a little over a month ago when she came back. She found out that the tumor was more aggressive and that she didn't have long to live which is why she was going to go to Brazil and marry some foreign man just to have the experience. But she couldn't do it. She left for only about a week and then she came back. She'd said that she wanted to die at home, around the few people that she knew cared about her."

"Why didn't you tell me?"

"She told me not to. She told me that you hated her and said that you never wanted to see or speak to her again, and she wanted you to have your wish. Your mother knew too because she made me bring her to the hospital so that she could apologize for lying on her husband. Your mama even went to the funeral with me. But she kept Patrice's wish and left it up to me to tell you."

Forget what I said, someone should have told me.

Patrice had betrayed me and lied to me, but at the end of the day I still had love for her.

And now I wouldn't be able to tell her that I forgive her.

"But she told me to tell you that she loved you. She said she always loved you. And nothing had changed that. And nothing ever would."

I wanted to cry but I didn't.

I should have requested to speak to Patrice the other day when she'd called Micki.

That was my chance and I'd missed it.

"Shall we proceed?"

"Why am I even here?"

"Well, according to this, Patrice left both of you everything. All of her money, straight down the middle."

I opened my mouth.

So did Micki.

I knew that she was going to ask and I waited for her to.

"How much?"

We both knew that Patrice had money.

From running her mother's clothing business she had made a fortune, on top of the fortune that he family already had.

"Twenty million dollars. A piece."

Micki damn near passed out.

I started to cry.

Even after all that, she had left me her money?

I just didn't know what to say.

"But there are conditions."

Micki and I looked at each other.

"Micki, you have always been a good friend. I love you so much and even all of this money can't express or show the love that I feel for you. But you need more. You need real love. You have a year to find it and marry it. And then you and your new husband and those bad ass kids of yours can enjoy all of this money together. Money means nothing without love. Money is nothing without family. Trust me, I know. Kisses to you from Heaven, or wherever the hell I am. You know that I had some things that needed to be forgiven so hopefully I make it in. I love you girl. Don't ever forget it." the lawyer read Patrice's last words to Micki.

Micki nodded and started to cry like a newborn baby.

The lawyer started to read again.

"Sassi, I love you. I'm so sorry I hurt you. If I could change what I did in the past I would...I didn't like his sex all that much anyway. I should have told you. But despite what I have said and despite that you think that Eddie is wrong for you, he is actually the right man for you Sassi. I couldn't see if before, but on my dying bed, and because Micki has kept me up to date with what's happening with you (You know that bitch can't keep a secret.

Except the one about me being sick, I hope) Eddie is the right one for you Sassi. Is it possible for love to be so wrong, yet so right at the same time? Absolutely. And is it possible for someone to be somewhat wrong for you, yet in some way be the best thing that ever happened to you? Sista' you are living proof. You have one year to make it work. I hear you are divorced well you better un-divorce then. Figure it out. You're smart. Put that big brain of yours to use and get your husband back. In a year you had better be married again, and then have him quit that new job of his. Take him back to Hawaii...and this time get pregnant. I love you. Oh, and P.S. here is some information for a publisher to publish your book when you get done with it. And you better finish. I took care of everything; and by that I mean I made a generous contribution to the publishing house for one of their new sub-companies. Legal agreement on file just in case. But when you are ready, she will publish your book for you. I know it's going to be good. I know it will be because I know you. Do me a favor, dedicate it to me why don't you. Hell, send a sista' a shout out to Heaven or something. I love you boo. Good bye Sassi...again."

The lawyer took a deep breath as Micki held me.

I was crying my eyes out.

Now I remembered why I loved her so much despite how big of a jerk she could be at times.

If only I had the chance to tell her that I loved her one last time.

After a few more minutes, and after the lawyer said that the money would be released to us, on this same day, a year later if we could provide documentation of marriage; Micki to anybody. Me, back to Eddie, Micki and I made our way back to the car.

We didn't say anything to each other.

If either of us failed to do what Patrice had in the will, our half would go to a charity of choice.

All of it.

I couldn't believe that Patrice had set me up a publishing deal and that she had left me so much money.

But she hadn't thought it all the way through.

How in the hell was I supposed to win Eddie back?

And get him to marry me again?

In a year?

I might as well kiss that money good bye because I already knew that wasn't going to happen.

But twenty million dollars?

That was a whole lot of money.

Too much to give up without a try.

Damn, I had twelve months to try to fix my situation and I didn't even know where to begin.

As we rode down the street, I looked up at the sky and imagined Patrice looking down on me from Heaven.

I managed to smile.

"Don't be up there giving Him a hard time, okay?"

I heard Micki slightly chuckle.

"I was just thinking the same thing."

****

CHAPTER 9

I had been writing my heart out.

I had so much on my mind and on my heart.

Patrice's death was weighing on me so heavily and I was still in somewhat a shock about it all.

"Do you need anything?"

Though I still Eddie's bad side, once I told him what happened with Patrice, he had been there for me, despite his personal feelings.

"I'm okay."

He nodded and headed back upstairs with the kids.

I hadn't told him what Patrice left in her will about the us or the money.

But her words had been ringing in my ear non-stop.

Though getting the money would be nice and we would be set for life, she was right about everything that she'd said about Eddie.

He may not have been everything I wanted but he was everything that I needed.

And I had to make it right.

I didn't want the money to influence his decision as to whether he should be with me again or not so I didn't tell him.

I was just going to work my ass off to win his heart back.

I just had to figure out how.

After calling him Polo's name, I knew that it was going to take damn near a miracle to get him to see that we were meant to be together, but I was desperate and I was willing to do anything.

Both for the love…and for the money.

Polo still hadn't really bothered me.

He'd called once or twice but that was about it.

Maybe he was going to leave me alone for good.

Maybe he was going on with his life.

I sure hope so.

If I was going to try to find a way to get Eddie back, Polo had to stay as far away from me as possible.

Hell maybe Eddie's idea to kill him should have been a real plan after all.

Things would definitely be better if we had.

But maybe there was another way to get rid of Polo.

I thought about the woman that he used to mess with; the one that had turned up dead.

It was weird that she died on the same day that she'd told me about the video tape that she saw of me and Polo.

At the time Polo was definitely into me and what we were doing behind Eddie's back, so maybe he had taken care of it himself.

Maybe he was angry at her for telling me.

Angry enough to kill her?

I wasn't so sure.

But with Polo, and his unstable personality, and if he was as crazy as Micki thought that he was, maybe he did do it.

Maybe I could find some evidence.

He only drove his jag, but he did have another car; a Cadillac Escalade, that he never drove and that no one hardly ever saw.

He kept it in that garage of his, and it was definitely big enough to knock the life out of someone, literally, even if he hadn't being going all that fast.

As far as I knew, they'd never found the person responsible for the hit and run.

Maybe I could check Polo's car for evidence.

Someway, somehow, he was going to have to go away, completely because I knew if Eddie and I tried to make something happen, he would surely try to mess it up.

He'd made that clear, so it was up to me to stop him.

~***~

"Mama, I want my husband back."

She and I were finally back on better terms.

"Go get him back then."

I knew that Eddie loved my mother as though he was her own and he respected her.

To him, she wasn't as much as a headache as his own, which was why initially he and the boys had gone to my mother's house instead when all of the crap with Polo and I hit the fan.

I knew that he would listen to anything that she had to say.

I knew that he would value her words of wisdom.

So, I needed her help.

I didn't inform her either about the money that Patrice had left behind or the restrictions that came with it.

"Can you talk to him for me?"

"And say what? The divorce is final now right?"

"Yes. But I think we can start over. I think that we still have a chance."

"And Polo?"

"Polo and I have nothing going on. Honestly, I haven't really seen or heard from him. Maybe he is on to the next, like his normal self."

"Was it really worth either of you losing the relationships that you had with Eddie?"

"No. If I miss what we had, I know that Polo has to miss their friendship terribly."

Mama shook her head.

Neither Polo or I could change the past, but I could try to change my future.

"Can you talk to him Mama? Please?"

She huffed.

"Tell me what to say and I will give it a try."

I smiled.

It was a start.

Speaking of the devil, just as Mama drove off, Polo pulled up beside me.

"Hey."

"Hey Polo."

"Oh, so we're back to being salty again?"

"No. I'm fine. What is it?"

"I just missed seeing your face."

"Polo, what huh? We aren't going to be together. We aren't going to have sex again, ever. So what huh?"

"Nothing Sassi. Like I told you, I'll always love you. And fine, move on. As long as you aren't with Eddie, I'm fine."

"Why though? Why not Eddie?"

"Because he was never supposed to have you. It was supposed to be me. And as I said, if I had to lose him, you have to lose him too."

Polo winked and drove off.

Yeah, my mind was made up.

His ass had to go.

Whether he was dead, in prison, or in somebody's crazy institution, Polo could consider himself soon to be a distant memory.

I was on a mission.

Rolling my eyes, I smiled as Micki pulled up next.

"Found a man yet?"

"Not one that I want to marry," Micki frowned.

She too was trying to get herself together and trying to find love so that she could get her share of the money.

"You know, in your case, you could just marry anyone," I said to her.

Hell, hers was simple.

Find someone, marry them, and get her money.

She didn't have to love them.

After they were married, they could divorce.

"Hmm, I didn't look at it that way. You are right. I could do that. I need that money."

As I said, Micki had always been a single mother.

She didn't really have help.

She wasn't a college graduate or anything, but she always kept some kind of job.

But things were always hard for her.

Manageable, but hard.

Twenty million dollars would change her whole life, and her kids.

"But I do only want to be married once; we will see. I'm on the hunt. If I can't find true love soon, I just may have to do what I got to do. I'm sure somebody will agree to marry me for the money. I'm just not comfortable with having to pay for a husband."

Micki talked a little while longer.

We both had a year to get our lives together.

But I wished my task was as easy as hers.

"Any luck with Eddie?"

"I haven't really tried. He's been around, but we don't talk about anything like that. I asked my Mama to try to talk to him and see where his head was. And then I guess I will go from there. I just don't want it to work for the money you know. Just like you. I really do want Eddie back. I really do want my life back."

"I know you do. Have you heard from Polo lately?"

"Yes, but nothing much. He's happy as long as Eddie and I aren't together."

"What kind of mess is that?"

"I don't know. You know Polo."

"I told you he was crazy. I told you."

Yeah.

And I was convinced that he was crazy enough to kill.

I had to make my way to his house so that I could be nosey.

I knew that it was something in that house that I could use against him.

I needed some kind of leverage.

I needed to find something that I could use to get rid of him for good.

Even if he hadn't committed the murder, there just had to be something that I could use.

I was sure that he had some kind of dirt or something.

Micki and I finished our conversation and I headed in the house to get the kids from Eddie.

"Hey."

"Hey."

"I love you."

"I see you guys tomorrow," Eddie said and headed out the door.

I rolled my eyes and chatted with the boys for a second.

After I got them settled with snacks and a movie, I sat on the couch and texted Eddie.

At first he didn't respond, but by the third text he asked me to stop saying that I loved him because I'd proved time and time again that I didn't.

But I did.

I really did.

I texted him a few more times and after he stopped responding I texted Mama and asked her to go ahead and give him a call.

And then I remembered that I'd blocked her cell number, so I had to text her and tell her to call from her house phone.

I grabbed a piece of paper and wrote down a plan.

I thought about everything that I knew about Eddie.

What he liked.

What he didn't.

What made him happy.

What made him smile.

Next I wrote down all I knew about Polo.

He was going down!

And I was going to make sure of that.

~***~

I waited for Polo to pull out and I prepared to make my move.

I didn't know where he was going so I had to get in and get out as soon as possible.

I'd taken Polo's house key off of Eddie's key ring the day before.

I knew exactly which one it was because I was the one that had put it on there and put a P on the back of it since it looked like so many other keys that we had.

I'd switched cars with my brother, just to make the run and I parked two houses up on the side of the road.

Polo had seen my brother's car before, but I doubted that he would pay it any attention.

As soon as he was out of sight, I got out of the car and headed towards Polo's house.

Looking around me, I put the key in the lock and turned the knob.

I walked in to the smell of men's cologne.

It smelled so good.

It smelled like Polo.

But I had to stay focused.

My first place was the garage so I headed to the door that led out to the garage from inside of the house.

I found the switch and walked towards the burgundy beauty on four wheels.

The car was shining and super clean.

I checked the front of it for any scratches or signs of blood but there was none.

There was nothing there that would hint that he could have been the driver behind the girl's accident.

Finally figuring that I should head to more rooms in the house, I turned off the light and headed to Polo's bedroom.

I had been in there plenty of times but I'd never had the chance to snoop around.

Polo was always there.

I didn't know where to start so I checked the closet.

He was so clean that I knew that I had to make sure that I put everything back in its proper place.

I didn't see anything so I came back out.

I looked on his dresser.

He had so many bottles of cologne, of the same exact kind.

There had to be about fifty bottles there.

Weirdo.

There was nothing out of place there though.

Nothing out of the ordinary.

I picked up one of the bottles of cologne just to give it a little spray.

Trying to pull the lid off of it, I dropped it and the lid rolled under the bed.

I got down on all fours to get it.

"What the hell…"

There were about ten boxes under the bed; along with wigs, hand cuffs and chains.

Not to mention a camcorder.

So he was videotaping us having sex?

Where?

How?

Of course the camcorder was a new updated, smaller one, so he could have stuck it pretty much anywhere that day and simply pressed record.

Even though I hadn't intentionally come to have sex with him, he must have been prepared, just in case.

I flipped through the saved recordings and sure enough there it was.

Excuse me, there they were.

There were several of recorded sexually encounters of us, starting from the first time, on up to the times that I was coming over during my lunch breaks.

And he'd named them…Sex with Sassi #1…Sex with Sassi #2…

He was such a sick little pervert!

I erased them all.

Every last one of them in a rage.

I started from the first time and on up.

There were tons of different recordings there and one other than mine, caught my attention.

Sex with Micki #1.

She'd told me that she hadn't had sex with Polo.

I pressed play and watched.

Polo started to undress her, but suddenly, she stopped him.

She started grabbing her things to leave and Polo got upset.

"I paid for it, and I want it."

After arguing for a while, she finally got away from him and ran out the door.

And then the video came to an end.

I guess she didn't sleep with him, but she'd planned to.

She'd been paid to, and I guess that's why Polo got upset and started doing all of those crazy things that she assumed that he did.

He was obsessive and definitely possessive and seeing how angry he was that she didn't keep the end of the deal, I was sure that he had been bothering her as a result of it.

I looked just to see if there were any from Patrice but there wasn't.

But there was one that said Eddie.

They were sitting in Polo's living room.

Judging from the angle, the camera had to be taping from somewhere near the fireplace mantel or maybe it was the bookcase that was right beside of it.

They talked for a while and then Eddie told him that he thought that I was cheating on him.

He told him that I had switched my panties and that he had a feeling that I was sleeping with someone else.

Polo tried to reason with him, knowing that he was the one that he was talking about.

And then Eddie said something else.

"I don't know what I would do if she was cheating on me man. I would probably die or try to kill her man," Eddie said.

Polo made a comment and then Eddie said.

"Or would you do it for me? Like last time."

What?

What the hell did he mean like last time?

Last time what?

Polo, assuming that he remembered that he was taping their conversation told Eddie that he was thinking crazy, and Eddie agreed that he was trippin' and wasn't thinking clearly.

He then invited him outside for a walk and that was it.

What did I just watch?

What did I just hear?

Was that somewhat a murder confession?

And Eddie was involved?

Or if he wasn't, he knew about it?

I wanted to listen to it again, but decided that I had been on the camcorder long enough.

Instead, I erased that video too.

You just never know what Polo might try to do with it.

I checked a few more of the boxes and they appeared to have things left behind from different women.

Panties, including the leopard ones of mine that he'd taken, lipstick, hair bows, things like that.

Another box was full of sex toys, gels and creams.

My mind was still on the fact that Eddie had mentioned something to Polo about killing me.

Hell, I guess I couldn't be all that surprised since he'd told me that he would if he could to my face on several occasions.

But what about the other comment?

Like you did before…

What had Polo done before?

And to who?

Though I wasn't done going through the boxes, I figured that I'd seen enough for one day and now that I knew where to look, I could come back another day.

I tried to straighten the boxes back up as they were.

I laid the camera down in the exact position as I'd found it.

I got the lid to the cologne and put it back on the bottle on the dresser.

It was time for me to get the hell out of here.

Just as I made it to the living room, I heard Polo talking.

Oh no!

He was outside of the door but I could hear him talking on the phone.

What was I going to do?

I needed to find somewhere to hide.

Wait a minute…

I had an idea.

I didn't like it, but it was the only choice that I had.

As I heard his keys, I took off my pants and my shirt and laid on the couch in just my bra and panties with my legs open.

Polo walked in.

I startled him and he dropped his phone.

Looking at me, he picked it up and said that he would call whoever it was back.

"Sassi?"

"I used Eddie's key to get in."

He looked at me.

"Um, where is your car?"

"I parked up the road just in case Eddie rode by or something."

Polo walked towards me with an evil grin on his face.

"Why are you here Sassi?"

Polo looked hungry.

Hungry for some of my good stuff.

I didn't want to have sex with Polo, but I knew that it was my only way out of this mess.

"What does it look like?"

Polo seemed unsure at first, but I knew that he wasn't going to turn me down.

He was undressed in a flash and let's just say that it was the longest twenty minutes of my life.

And it was the first time, the only time, that I hadn't enjoyed sex with Polo.

~***~

"We never really talked about why it happened," I said to Eddie.

"It doesn't matter why Sassi. What matters is that it did."

"But can you hear me out? For once without getting mad? Without walking away or cutting me off? Could you just let me tell you?"

I could tell that Eddie didn't want to hear it, but he nodded his head anyway.

"I felt like something was missing. You were always good to me, but over the years you changed. We didn't have fun. We didn't seem to have a lot in common."

"Then all you had to do was say that Sassi."

"I tried so many times, but you didn't get it. It just seemed like we didn't fit. We had great teamwork, but still yet, emotionally, even socially, it just seemed as though we weren't the perfect match. And this was before the sex issues that I had been feeling that way Eddie. It wasn't just as a result of the sex issue, no matter what you think."

"We could have gone to counseling or something Sassi. I was going through things too but I wasn't sleeping around on you. Hell my business was flopping and I didn't even know how to tell my wife because I didn't want you to be disappointed in me. I didn't want to let you down. So I was working overtime, anytime, hard just to try to make things work. But I failed anyway. I felt like a failure. And then to find out that you were sleeping with Polo, it all almost made me snap Sassi. I could have really hurt you."

His comment reminded me of what I saw on Polo's camcorder.

"You were mad enough to kill me Eddie? Like for real?"

"Hell yeah! I mean I wanted you and whoever the man was dead because I knew that I was trying to be the best husband that I could be. And then when I found out that it was Polo. I didn't want to believe. I just didn't want to accept it. When I came there with the gun that day, I wanted to shoot both of you. I think I would have had not a quick memory of you having our first child crossed my mind. I have no idea why it did at that moment, but it did, and that's the only reason that I didn't shoot you Sassi."

Well, at least he was honest.

But what about the other comment that he had made to Polo about him doing it before?

What was that all about?

I wanted to ask, but I knew that Eddie wouldn't tell me.

At least not right now.

"Why Polo Sassi?"

I took a deep breath.

"He was there. He was easy access. He told me his feelings for me and I allowed them to actually mean something to me because I wasn't happy. Even though I wanted to be happy, I wasn't."

Eddie didn't say anything.

"I never meant to ruin your friendship with Polo or our marriage. I allowed things to go too. I could have stopped them but I didn't."

"Both of you are at fault. But you know what, I forgive you and Polo. Polo and I can never go back to being how we were and you and I may never have what we had, but I forgive you. I have to forgive you for me. I'm tired of being angry Sassi. I talked to your mother and she made me realize that holding on the hurt only continues to hurt the person feeling the pain, while the people that hurt you are moving on with their lives."

"But I'm not moving on Eddie. It took me losing you to realize that I lost the best part of me."

"I just don't believe that Sassi."

"But it's true. You have to still love me Eddie."

"I'll always love you Sassi, but that's just not enough."

We both stopped talking and just sat there.

I tried to think of something that I could say that might have a big impact on him or pull at his heart strings.

Then I thought of something.

"We both did things. You lied to me. I lied and betrayed you. But remember what we said when we took our vows? We'd said until death do us part, and you told me that no matter what I did and no matter what happened, that the only way that you would leave me was if you "woke up dead". You said that you would literally have to die in your sleep because any other way, you would have found a way to live, you would have found a way to keep breathing, just for me. Remember?"

Eddie looked down at the floor.

"Now we're sitting here divorced and I don't want to be. I still love you, and I know that I messed up big time but I need for you to keep your promise to me. I need to you to keep your vow even though I broke a part of mine."

Eddie was speechless.

I could tell that he had a million things going on in his head.

"The second time around is always better. It's always sweeter they say. Things will be different and better, I just know that they will."

I had to get Eddie back.

And I was going to do it.

One day.

One memory.

One word at a time.

~***~

"You wouldn't dare."

"Oh, but I would."

Polo threatened to tell Eddie that we'd just had sex again

I'd talked Eddie into going out to dinner with me.

Well, I'd talked him into taking me out to eat since he was the one with the job.

Polo must have a tracking device or something on one of us because out of nowhere, he popped up.

He texted me and told me to meet him near the bathroom.

"We are just having a meal."

"Looks like y'all are trying to work things out to me, but just the other day I had your legs up in the air and you were screaming my name."

Oh how I wanted to tell him that I faked it.

But I knew that would piss him off and he would surely tell Eddie.

"He won't believe you."

Polo laughed.

He walked off and headed for Eddie and I followed him.

"Bro, long time no see," Polo said.

Eddie cringed.

"I'm not your bro Polo. My brother wouldn't have done what you did with my wife."

"Are we still on that? I thought we got past that."

"What is it Polo?"

"I just wanted to come over and see how you have been. I saw Sassi the other day, but I forgot to ask about you."

Eddie looked at me.

"What day was that Sassi? The day that you had on that red shirt and those killer white pants?"

Of course Eddie had seen me that day, so he knew that Polo had seen me too.

Polo opened his mouth and just as he did, in a panic, I picked up the wine bottle off of the table and hit him with it.

Polo fell to the floor, knocked out cold.

Everyone gasped.

"What the hell is wrong with you Sassi? Why did you do that?" Eddie jumped.

"I'm tired of him bothering us Eddie. He just needs to leave me alone. Leave us alone."

Really I'd hit him to keep him from telling him that we'd had sex.

It was the only thing that I knew to do.

The restaurant staff rushed over but Eddie told him that he had everything under control.

He said that Polo was a friend of ours and that it had been an accident.

He explained that I had a disorder and I'd thought that Polo was trying to attack me while having one of my spells.

Eddie shook Polo.'

Polo opened his eyes.

"Eddie?"

"Yeah man, let's get you out of here. See, he knows me," Eddie said to them and he helped Polo up and headed for the door.

I followed behind them, still holding the bottle.

"I'll drive him home, you follow behind us in my car."

I wished that the blow to the head had killed him.

But that would have been too easy and my life just wasn't set up that way.

We pulled up at Polo's house and by then Eddie had told Polo that some girl that he probably used to sleep with came out of nowhere and hit him in the back of the head with a bottle.

Polo was still shaken up and with the knot growing on his head, Eddie suggested the hospital, but Polo refused.

He glanced at me in the car, but Polo didn't say anything.

Eddie helped him into the house and after some time, he came back out.

I got out and headed to the passenger side.

"Sassi, that was crazy!"

"Ever since whatever he has been giving me such a hard time. Harassing me. Popping up. Calling me all the time. I told him over and over again that it was a mistake and I just want him to go away."

"You caused all of this. We all were fine. We had good friendships, we were married. But you chose to sleep with Polo."

"I know. Can you fix it for me? It was a horrible mistake, can you fix it Eddie?"

"What?"

"What is it that you know on Polo? Who did he kill Eddie?"

"What? What are you talking about Sassi?"

"Polo recorded a conversation between you and him. You told him that you thought that I was cheating. You said that if you found out that I was that you were going to kill me. And then you asked Polo could he do it for you…like he did before. Who did he kill Eddie?"

Eddie looked as though he couldn't believe the words coming out of my mouth.

"Never repeat that again Sassi. Ever."

"What did he do before Eddie? To who?"

"Sassi, just let it go. There's no point in going digging around in past things that you have nothing to do with. I'll make sure that Polo leaves you alone from here on out okay? Just don't ever mention that again."

Eddie drove like a bat out of hell down the street.

I turned to look out the window and smiled.

Honestly, I didn't care what it was; if Eddie could get Polo to leave me alone completely, then screw the little secret that they had.

I was just fine with that.

~***~

"I finished it," I squealed in Micki's ear.

My book was finish and I didn't know what to do with myself.

"I'm so proud of you."

"Thank you."

"Now what, do you reach out to the company from the Patrice's will?"

"Yeah. I guess that's the next step. Speaking of, found someone to start dating yet?"

"Actually, I did. He's a white guy. We had our first date the other day. He wants kids and a wife, so I'm hoping that we hit it off. And you?"

"Girl, I'm gonna need more than a few weeks to break Eddie down. But we did have sex again the other day. We were both just horny I guess. But he's still not bending all that much."

"It'll work out."

"I hope so. But someone's ringing the doorbell so I will call you back."

I got up off of the toilet, got myself together and ran down the stairs.

I opened it.

"Eddie, why didn't you just use you key?"

He looked at me as though I'd asked a stupid question.

"I couldn't get to it obviously."

He was carrying both of the boys.

They were both asleep.

He carried them in, laid them on the couch and started to undress them.

"Sassi, what if I came to stay here? Like a roommate or something. I'm always here. I'll sleep down here on the couch.

My folks are driving me crazy. I'll start looking for a place as soon as possible. I won't be here longer than a month."

"Yes."

With him under the same roof as me and the kids, I was going to work some magic.

I was going to make Eddie never want to leave.

I was going to get my husband back.

And twenty million dollars too.

Eddie carried the oldest upstairs first.

Once he came back down, I made a suggestion.

"You know you miss us. Let's just work it out Eddie."

"I don't know Sassi. I just don't know."

He picked up our smallest child and then he carried him upstairs too.

In my thoughts, I thought about how many ways I could seduce him and how many ways I could tempt him and make him remember why he loved me and wanted to marry me in the first place.

Wrong husband originally or not, he was all I ever needed.

And I had twenty million reasons that would cosign to that.

A knock at the door stole my attention.

I figured it was Mama since she was supposed to stop by but I was wrong.

It was Polo.

I frowned but he smiled.

He walked right in my house without an invite.

"Excuse me?"

"Eddie told me to meet him here."

What?

"Eddie!" I screamed.

"Why?"

"I don't know Sassi."

"I would appreciate it if you didn't tell him about…"

Polo nodded behind me to Eddie standing on the steps.

He walked down the few that he had left to go, slowly.

He walked directly in front of me.

He held up his hand.

Damn it!

I had been taking a pregnancy test while on the phone with Micki and had left it on the sink.

I totally forgot about it.

I hadn't had a period in a while and figured that it was time to test.

"You're pregnant Sassi. Is it mine? Or is it Polo's?"

I looked back and forth between both of them.

Though originally I was trying to put the baby on Eddie, no matter what, at that moment, and looking at the positive pregnancy test, I had another plan.

Eddie looked at the test, and Polo looked at me.

I took a deep breath.

"It's not mine."

Of course it was mine, but they didn't have to know that.

"What?"

"It's Micki's. She was here earlier and she took a pregnancy test. We started talking while we were waiting for the results and forgot all about it," I lied.

Eddie looked at me.

Polo was staring at me too as though he was trying to decide whether he believe me or not.

"Look, I'll prove it."

I grabbed my phone to call Micki.

She knew I was taking a test and she would lie for me and fall in line with the story with little to no details.

That's what friends were for.

The phone ranged and I looked as the sound of her phone ringing came through the front door.

Micki.

"I was just calling you. Tell them that the pregnancy test it yours," I said to her.

She didn't say anything.

She walked over and stood beside Polo.

All three of them seemed very strange at that moment and I felt uneasy.

Suddenly, Eddie spoke.

"She knows."

"Knows what?" Polo asked.

"Vanessa."

Micki and Polo gasped.

What?

Who and the hell is Vanessa?

I didn't know a Vanessa and I didn't have a clue as to what they were talking about.

"How?" I was surprised to hear Micki ask.

"She said she watched a recording of a conversation that Polo and I had."

Polo looked at Eddie and then at me.

"Damn, you're nosey."

"What the hell is going on? What are y'all talking about? Who is Vanessa?"

I turned to face Eddie.

Micki walked over and stood beside him and out of nowhere, Polo grabbed me from behind.

What?

He somewhat placed me in a choke hold.

It wasn't too tight where he was choking me but it was tight enough where I couldn't get out of it.

"Get the hell off of me Polo! Eddie? Micki? Get him off of me!"

But they both just stood there.

What the hell is happening right now?

I squirmed for a few minutes more and then Polo took his free hand and it was though he was searching for something on my neck.

He found the spot, and pressed firmly on some kind of pressure point, that I didn't even know that I had.

I felt woozy all of a sudden and my eyes became heavy as Polo continued to hold me and press down.

I was passing out.

Or I guess Polo was causing me to pass out in some way.

My body became limp and I could no longer try to get away from Polo.

Closing my eyes, Eddie and Micki started to talk and then suddenly, I didn't see them.

I didn't hear them.

Everything was quiet.

Everything was dark.

Uh oh.

TO BE CONTINUED

****

Made in the USA
Columbia, SC
26 February 2019